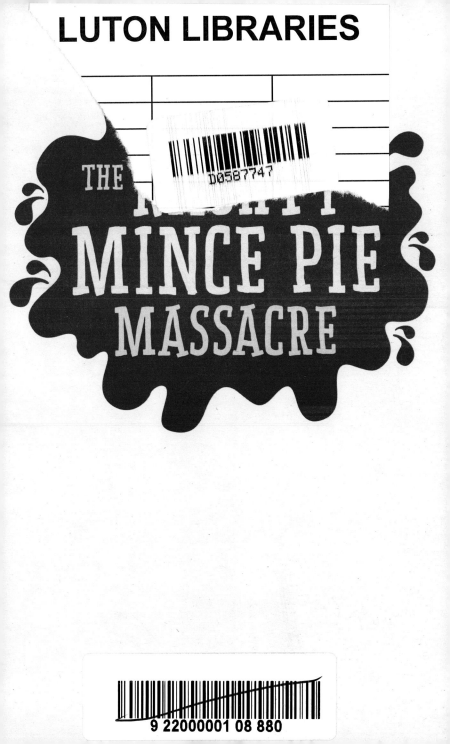

THE MIGHTY
MINCE PIE
MASSACRE

BY MARK LOWERY

The Roman Garstang Adventures

The Jam Doughnut that Ruined My Life
The Chicken Nugget Ambush
Attack of the Woolly Jumper
The Great Caravan Catastrophe
Revenge of the Spaghetti Hoops

Charlie & Me

THE MIGHTY MINCE PIE MASSACRE

MARK LOWERY

Piccadilly
PRESS

First published in Great Britain in 2018 by
PICCADILLY PRESS
80–81 Wimpole St, London W1G 9RE
www.piccadillypress.co.uk

Text copyright © Mark Lowery, 2018
Illustrations copyright © Cherie Zamazing, 2018

A CIP catalogue record for this book
is available from the British Library.

ISBN: 978-1-84812-731-9
Also available as an ebook

1

Typeset by Palimpsest Book Production Ltd, Falkirk, Stirlingshire
Printed and bound by Clays Ltd, Elcograf S.p.A.

Piccadilly Press is an imprint of Bonnier Zaffre Ltd,
part of Bonnier Books UK
www.bonnierbooks.co.uk

For Sarah, Minnie, Sam and Doogs

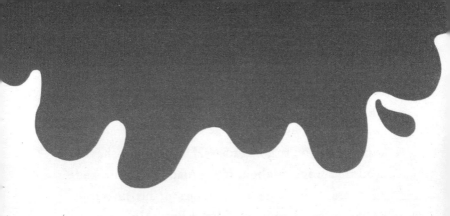

I hate mince pies.

I don't know how anyone could like them. They're the worst thing about Christmas by an absolute mile.

OK, so a lot of people would say Brussels sprouts are worse. I agree that sprouts *are* horrible – they taste like old socks and they make you parp like a brass band. But at least sprouts are honest about how grim they are. They're *green* for a start. And everyone knows that all green things are bad: mould, stinging nettles, salad.

In fact, sprouts are a bit like my so-called best friend, Darren Gamble. Yes, Gamble can occasionally blow things up, or tip head lice into your mashed potato, or kick the odd horse here and there. But he's not mean or crafty about it – he just can't help himself.

Plus he *looks* naughty as well, so you always know what you're going to get. He has a tiny shaved head that waggles about like a mad jelly bean, and he wears T-shirts with the names of his favourite heavy metal bands on the front. His current favourite bands are called: The Sweaty Mums, Attack of the Sabre-Toothed Butt Squirrels, and Dog Dirt Dave and the Poop-a-Scoops.

Mince pies, on the other hand, are tricky little con artists. From the outside, they make you think they're quite nice: little parcels of crumbly pastry with icing sugar sprinkled on the top like a light dusting of snow.

Yum yum.

To look at them, you'd think they could be stuffed with anything: jam, chocolate, Skittles.

But they aren't.

They're full of this brown, lumpy gunk. It's *called* 'mincemeat' but nobody on earth knows what it *really* is. There's no meat in there and it tastes disgusting. Mum says that mincemeat is just raisins and other dried fruit in a sweet, spicy sauce. To me, it tastes more like rabbit droppings mixed with the sludge that fat men get in between their rolls of flab.

Mince pies are very similar to this girl in my class called Rosie Taylor (AKA the worst person who has ever existed in the history of the universe). Some people think Rosie is a good person, but I know better. She can be all nicey-nice when it suits her, but really she's cruel and she completely hates my guts. She's got a tiny little mouth like a hamster's nipple, which she mainly uses to say cruel things about me. She once spread a rumour that I have a 'bright purple bum like a baboon', and last year on her birthday she made a wish that I'd get eaten alive by 'wild toddlers'.

When you think about it, mince pies have also got a lot in common with actors.

That's right, actors: those idiots who star in plays and TV shows and films. People think they're really special and glamorous and *amaaaaaaaaazing*.

But they aren't.

You can't trust actors at all. Their lives are just one big lie. Remember: their job is to pretend to be other people. From the outside, they seem exciting, but that's only because you think they're someone else – a princess, a blood-sucking zombie, a superhero. When you find out who they really are, you realise that they're totally rubbish.

Maybe you think I'm being cruel to actors and mince pies. Well, you're wrong. Last Christmas, I spent way too much time with an actor, and ate way too many mince pies.

The results were catastrophic.

SUNDAY

Gamble Gets Involved in a Play and Mrs McDonald Has Some Time Off Work

It probably seemed like a good idea at the time. A nice pre-Christmas treat for the class: a Sunday evening trip to the theatre.

Our Christmas school play was coming up at the end of the week. Before then, Mrs McDonald wanted us to see a proper, professional panto. She wanted us to be inspired, and make our performance on Friday better. So she organised for us all to meet at the theatre on Sunday night.

I'm not really sure *why* she bothered to take us in the first place. What was the point? Our class had one short song-and-dance to do in the school Christmas production. We were only going to be onstage for three minutes. Maybe she shouldn't have taken us at all.

Still, there was no way she could've known what would happen.

FACT 1: most people who go to a panto don't get crushed by a man dressed as a woman, then set on fire by a pair of exploding fake boobs.

FACT 2: if you *do* get set on fire by a pair of fake boobs, that's usually the worst thing that could happen to you that week. Things don't normally get worse AFTERWARDS.

Mince Pie

'Best seats in the house!' said Mrs McDonald, cheerfully leading us to the front row of the theatre. The room was filling up, and there was a fizz of excitement in the air, like when someone lights the fuse on a firework. 'We'll be almost close enough to *touch* the actors onstage.'

I'd soon learn that this wasn't actually a good thing.

I was just about to plop myself onto my seat when Darren Gamble slithered out from under it. 'Sit on me and I'll eat your bum.'

'What are you doing down there?' I said.

I'm amazed that Darren Gamble is allowed to go on school trips after all the things he's done – like the zoo visit when he stripped off naked and punched that penguin. Or at the history museum when he played football with an Ancient Egyptian mummy's head.

His bulging eyes flicked from side to side. 'I'm proper excited for the start of the play, innit.'

I frowned. 'Have you been drinking your energy drink again?'

Grinning, he held up a can of drink that read:

**FLAPPING TERROR
EXTREME ENERGY DRINK
Because sleeping is for dead people
WARNING: May cause blindness, explosions
of the heart and some melting of the skull.**

'That looks like pretty strong stuff,' I said uneasily. Darren's behaviour is always even worse when he's been chugging on energy drinks.

'Yep. Well strong. They use it to dissolve batteries in Kazakhstan.'

'Oh.'

I looked around for somewhere else to sit.

'Hey, please don't leave,' whined Gamble. 'You're my best mate ever and I love you.'

'Oh,' I said. 'That's . . . *kind*.'

He sniffed. 'And if you try to move I'll give you a volcanic-nuclear-terror-wedgie until your head bursts.'

I gulped. That didn't sound very nice. Reluctantly, I slid into my seat.

'What treats have you got then?' Gamble said, plonking himself next to me and bouncing up and down.

'None.'

Gamble punched me in the arm. 'Don't lie. You don't go anywhere without snacks. I've seen you bring a jam doughnut into assembly before.'

I sighed. This was true. That assembly had been an extra-long one though. And some people *do* say I have a bit of a doughnut habit. Well, if you call twelve doughnuts per day a habit, that is. Personally, I call it a hobby.

I reached into my coat and pulled out the bag of Fruit Pastilles I'd pinched from home.

'My favourites!' exclaimed Gamble. 'Plus they've got fruit in so they're probably one of your five a day.'

'Mn-yeah. They're OK. We'd run out of doughnuts,' I said. In other words, I'd eaten eight in one go and Mum had refused to buy any more 'until you've thought about what you've done'.

Gamble wiped his nose on his sleeve. 'Wanna swap? I've brought a mince pie. It's proper Christmassy, innit.'

'I'd rather n—' I began but Gamble snatched the bag out of my hand and shoved the mince pie in its place.

Great.

I've already said I don't like mince pies, but this

one was particularly unappetising. It was small, and burnt round the edges, and the pastry was kind of *sweaty*. Also it smelled quite strongly of Gamble (imagine a dead fish stuffed with an old man's undies and you're halfway there).

I stared at it and gulped.

'Ain't you gonna eat it?' he asked. His voice was just a little bit threatening.

'I might save it till later . . .'

Like, twenty years later perhaps.

'What's wrong with it?' he asked. 'My mum made that. If you don't eat it, I'll twist off your eyebrows.'

'It's still a bit warm,' I said. 'I don't want to burn my mouth.'

Gamble sniffed. 'It's only warm cos it's been in my pocket.'

Delightful.

'Maybe we could swap back . . . ?' I asked hopefully.

'Eat it. Now!'

I took a tiny nibble and nearly fainted. It tasted like a mix between burnt car tyres and soil.

'Wow. That is . . . *powerful*!' I said, my eyes watering. 'What's in it?'

'Duh. Mince,' he replied. 'It's a *mince* pie, innit.'

I raised one eyebrow. Like I said before, *nobody* knows what mincemeat really is. The confident expression on Gamble's face made me feel very worried. 'Er . . . What *kind* of mince?'

'Hedgehog,' smiled Gamble. 'Dad squashed it in the car and mum minced it up and put it in a pie.'

GROSS! I spat it out into a tissue.

Things Get Worse

At that moment, Gamble's teaching assistant, Miss Clegg, flopped down on the other side of me. I don't want to be horrible, but Miss Clegg is quite a large person. The side of her body was oozing over the arm-rest like a sack of yoghurt.

By the way, you might wonder why she was sitting next to me and not Gamble. After all, she's *his* teaching assistant; she's supposed to look after him and keep him out of trouble.

The truth is simple: she hates him and she's terrible at her job. Any chance she gets to avoid him, she takes it. One time she had to drive him to hospital because he fainted after eating a permanent marker pen. Instead of waiting with him, she tipped him onto the pavement outside A & E with a note that read: *Beware: may bite if woken suddenly.*

'Who's got mince pies?' she said, sniffing the air. 'I'll have a mince pie.'

I held the rest of it out to her. She swooped in like a hawk, snatched it up out of my hand and gobbled it down whole. Then she pulled out the biggest bag of crisps I've ever seen (honestly the size of a large suitcase) and started noisily shoving great fistfuls of them down her gob right next to my ear. It was terrible, like listening to a bunch of hyenas crunching up a zebra.

I sighed. With Gamble bouncing around on one side of me and her guzzling away on the other, this was going to be a long, long evening.

But I had no idea quite how bad things would get.

A sharp fingernail tapped me on the shoulder. 'Excuse me, Roman.' The voice was slow and slimy, like a snake tightening around my neck.

Rosie Taylor. Just what I needed.

I turned around to look at her. 'Are you OK?'

Rosie pursed her hamster's nipple mouth at me. 'Your massive head's in the way. We're here so that everyone else can learn to be as magnifitabulous at acting as I am. How can they if your giant melon is blocking the whole stage?'

I rolled my eyes.

Rosie is always being mean to me. Last year she tried to sell my brain on eBay. The advert read: *For Sale – Useless Blob of Gunge. Might make good slug food.* Nobody bought it. I wasn't sure if this was a good thing or a bad thing.

Rosie continued. 'You need to duck down or maybe just cut your head off. *Hashtag:* pass the rusty saw. Let's make this as painful as possible.'

I sighed. 'And a Merry Christmas to you too.'

'It will be,' Rosie sneered, 'if I get the present I've asked for.'

'And what's that?'

Rosie clapped her hands together excitedly. 'For you to get electrocuted by fairy lights, or mashed up and cooked in a Christmas pudding, or eaten by a reindeer or . . .'

I turned to the front. Could this experience get any more unpleasant?

Of course it could.

'Hey, Roman!'

The voice was coming from above.

I looked up. Kevin Harrison was sitting directly above me, leaning over the edge of the balcony rail. Kevin is always throwing up, which is why his nickname is *Vomasaurus Retch*. Trust me, he's the last person you want sitting ten feet above your head.

'What are you doing up there?' I asked.

'My parents wanted to come as well, so we got tickets together in the royal box,' he said. His mum and dad peered over the rail and waved.

I waved back. 'Royal box? Sounds nice.'

'Oh yeah!' exclaimed Kevin. 'You get free food and drink. I've had six Cornettos and three massive bottles of Fanta!'

'Lovely,' I said, swallowing hard.

So not only was I sandwiched between Gamble and Miss Clegg, with the worst person ever sitting right behind me, I now had a ticking time bomb of puke above me, stuffed full of fizzy drinks and ice cream and just waiting to explode. Things were getting worse by the second.

Right then the lights in the room went down.

'Hush, everyone!' hissed Mrs McDonald. 'And watch carefully. We're here to learn.'

She was right – I would learn a lot. Unfortunately

I would mainly learn how to put on a terrible, awful, disaster of a play, and exactly how dangerous exploding fake boobs can be.

The Panto

The panto was *Jack and the Beanstalk* but I have no idea if Jack actually went up the beanstalk or not. It finished way before he'd even got hold of the magic beans.

The first scene didn't make a lot of sense to me. Jack was played by a grown-up woman actor, dressed as a boy. His mum (Madame Boom Boom) was played by a man actor, wearing a towering blue wig, bright pink dress and outrageous make-up. The cow was played by two humans who might've been men or women but definitely weren't cows.

Typical actors, I thought, *they can never just be themselves*.

Madame Boom Boom was called this because every time she came onstage, her two enormous fake boobs would both explode in a big flash of light. I've no idea why this happened but it was pretty funny. The first time, Gamble laughed so hard that his face went blue and Flapping Terror shot out of his nostrils.

It was shortly after this that the real problems began.

Old Pants

Madame Boom Boom had just started a song and dance routine. The song was all about how poor she and Jack were. It was called 'I Can't Even Afford New Knickers'.

The words were really rude:

> *I've owned these ancient drawers,*
> *Since the time of the dinosaurs.*
> *They're full of stains and skids*
> *That are older than the pyramids.*
> *And they completely fall apart*
> *Every time I do a . . .*

You can probably guess the rest.

As she sang, she danced off the stage and into the audience with her washing basket, taking out different pairs of comedy undies and waving them about. There were feathery ones, lacy ones, red ones, white ones, and saggy old grey ones that were roughly the size of China.

Gamble wasn't watching her though. He was too busy straining to open the Fruit Pastilles. His face was bright red as he yanked on the bag with his puny arms.

By now, Madame Boom Boom was right in front of us, holding up a pair of enormous pink frilly bloomers.

'Is it such a terrible THAAAAAANG?' she wailed. The music paused and she took a deep breath, clutching the knickers to her enormous chest. 'To want some pants that aren't as old as the big BAAAAAAAANNNNNNNNNNNG!'

This was the big finale. As she belted out the last note, the music got louder and louder. The audience began to cheer. Catherine wheels spun round on her boobs, firing sparks in every direction.

And the bag of Fruit Pastilles burst EVERYWHERE.

Then Tragedy Struck

As soon as they hit the floor, Gamble was already after them. He was amazing! He had his mouth open and he was sucking them up directly off the carpet like a Hoover.

Most of them were in his mouth by the time the applause had died down and Madame Boom Boom was back up on the stage. 'So you see, Jack, my lad,' she said to her son, who was really a girl, 'we need some money fast or my kecks will have worn as thin as that cow over there.'

The cow mooed sadly.

Then everything went very wrong.

'Oi!' yelled Gamble, pointing at Madame Boom Boom's foot. He was on all fours on the floor, and his cheeks were full of half-chewed pastilles, like some disgusting rodent. Everybody in the theatre seemed to turn towards us. Up on the stage, I could just about see a couple of Fruit Pastilles stuck to the bottom of Madame Boom Boom's clumpy boots. 'She's just robbed me, she has! Give us back them sweets, you massive ape.'

The audience muttered to each other.

'Darren, please,' said Mrs McDonald from along the row.

'Yeah, Darren. Stop, or something,' yawned Miss Clegg, lazily tipping the rest of her crisps into her mouth.

Onstage, a look of irritation flashed across Madame Boom Boom's face. 'I do apologise, ladies and gentlemen,' she said gruffly. 'The goose isn't meant to appear until later in the show. But it appears one of its turds has dropped down from the clouds and landed in the audience.'

I thought this was way too cruel, but a couple of people laughed. I didn't. And neither did Gamble. The last thing anyone should ever do is wind him up.

He let out a savage roar. Then he erupted off the floor and bounded onto the stage in front of the whole audience. He grabbed Madame Boom Boom by the ankle, twisted her foot round and tried to eat the Fruit Pastilles directly off the bottom of her boot.

It was chaos. The actors onstage had stopped acting completely. Jack and the back half of the cow were trying to pull Gamble off, while Madame Boom Boom was kicking out at him and howling, 'Gerrim off me!'

The other actors finally managed to yank Gamble away. He fell backwards, still holding onto Madame Boom Boom's clumpy boot, which came off with a *plop*. This caused Madame Boom Boom to stagger forward to the edge of the stage. She struggled to balance there on one leg for a moment, arms whirling round like a giant baby bird. Then she toppled forward and landed face first on top of Mrs McDonald.

Everyone in the room went, 'Ooooh!' Some people clapped, thinking it was still part of the show. Mrs McDonald was trying to wrestle this great heavy man-woman off her and whimpering for help. Miss Clegg was filming it on her mobile phone.

Then tragedy struck.

BANG! BANG!

Madame Boom Boom's boobs exploded again.

There was a yelp of pain from Mrs McDonald. Madame Boom Boom rolled off her and landed in a heap in the aisle, which revealed something absolutely terrifying.

Mrs McDonald was on fire.

It was awful. Flames were licking up off her cardigan. She flapped at them but they were now spreading rapidly across her body.

'Someone do something!' cried Rosie Taylor. 'If those flames go near me they could ruin my good looks.'

I said nothing. Rosie thinks she's beautiful, but actually she's got a face like a miserable goat.

Fortunately someone *did* do something to put out the flames.

*Un*fortunately, it was Kevin *Vomasaurus Retch* Harrison.

I don't want to go into too much detail, but let's just say that he put the fire out using his own special skills. There was a loud splash, then a hissing, sizzling sound, and a smell like burning Cornetto mixed with sour orange juice.

Madame Boom Boom staggered back onto the stage and the curtain came down behind her. Gamble crawled out from under it, leaped down and sat next to me again. 'Got my sweets back, innit,' he grinned, opening his mouth to show me. 'Let's get on with the play.'

But the play was over.

The lights came on. For a moment the whole theatre was silent, apart from Gamble chewing and Mrs McDonald quietly weeping.

Rosie Finds a Replacement

Twenty minutes later, we were standing outside the theatre as Mrs McDonald was loaded into an ambulance. The rest of the audience had taken the cancellation of the play really well. Of course, by 'really well' I mean they'd booed and jeered and thrown things at our group as they left the theatre. I'd been hit on the side of the head with a Twix ice cream, which wasn't very friendly.

Gamble was now wearing reins, with Miss Clegg holding the other end. The paramedics had insisted that he was kept away so they could do their job. When Gamble had realised that Mrs McDonald was injured, he'd tried to give her a blood transfusion by picking off a scab and thrusting his bleeding elbow at her mouth. He'd then clamped onto her leg like burnt spaghetti at the bottom of a pan, until Miss Clegg peeled him off.

For some reason, Gamble loves Mrs McDonald. Or at least he loves her in the same way that a deranged one-year-old holding a heavy rock might love a ladybird.

The ambulance edged away with its lights flashing. Gamble slipped out of his reins, ran behind and jumped up onto the back bumper.

'Oh, stop. You could get hurt,' said Miss Clegg, as the ambulance sped away with Gamble clinging on. I'm not sure she should have been smiling quite so much when she said this.

Nobody seemed to know what to do next.

'*Hashtag*: how selfish!' said Rosie Taylor.

I turned around slowly to face her. 'Eh? Who's selfish?'

'Mrs McDonald, you frightful little mutant,' said Rosie, looking me up and down. 'Oh, and your parents, for not putting you in a zoo when you were born.'

I ignored this last bit. 'Why is Mrs McDonald being selfish?'

Rosie rolled her eyes. 'Er . . . Let me think. The Christmas play is on Friday. It's going to be an absolute embarrassment if we don't practise properly. And now Mrs McDonald's gone and set herself on fire.'

'I don't think she did it on purpose,' I said, but Rosie clearly wasn't listening.

I mean, *I'm* obvs perfectalicious already,' she continued, preening her hair. 'But – no offence – the rest of you look and sound like a bunch of drunk giraffes falling down the stairs.'

I tried not to laugh but I couldn't help myself. Rosie thinks she's the most talented person on earth. I've seen jars of snot with more talent than her.

Rosie didn't like this. 'You can laugh. But I'm

going to record the performance on Friday and send it off to Hollywood film directors, so I can be a professional actress.'

'Good luck with that,' I said. With Rosie's singing, dancing and acting ability, she could easily get a part in a film. She could play something really important, like a bag of broken alarm clocks, or a tub of melted cheese.

'Well,' said Rosie, 'my daddy will sort this out. He's super-rich and he's a school governor. So he's literally the most important person on earth.'

'That's a bit of an exaggeration,' I said. 'Don't the school governors just help to run the school?'

Rosie ignored me. 'He'll make sure that Mrs McDonald's replacement is someone who will make this performance on Friday amazing.'

With that, she swept away and began rabbiting into her mobile phone. 'Daddy. Stop what you're doing . . . No, I don't care if you're in a meeting. Your princess needs you . . .'

MONDAY

Mrs McDonald Is Replaced and We Become Professional Actors

On Monday morning Mr Noblet was waiting for us in the classroom. Mr Noblet is our head teacher. Everyone likes him, even though he does have a moustache. Moustaches are awful – they're like beards for people who can't be bothered. Mr Noblet's is really bushy and makes him look like he's balancing a sea lion on his upper lip.

'Take a seat, guys,' he said. 'Darren, could you stop chewing through that electrical wire? I think it's actually plugged into the wall . . .'

'Soz, sir,' said Gamble. 'I was up late in the hospital with Mrs McDonald, innit, and I've run out of Flapping Terror. I thought I should electrocute myself. You know. To wake myself up.'

'Oh,' said Mr Noblet. He looked like he wasn't sure if Gamble was joking or not. I could've told him that he wasn't. 'So how was Mrs McDonald?'

Gamble scratched his bald skull. 'Dunno, sir. They kicked me out of the ward when I started drinking out of someone's drip, so I ended up hanging out in the big freezer.'

'The big . . . *freezer*?'

'You know, sir – where they keep the dead people.'

Mr Noblet's eyes nearly popped out of his head. 'Good grief.'

'Must've been nice to find some people who didn't find you utterly disgusting,' yawned Miss Clegg.

'Shut it, you sweaty butt flicker,' snapped Gamble.

I've no idea what a sweaty butt flicker is, but it seemed to fit Miss Clegg quite well.

'Shall we move on?' said Mr Noblet, looking a bit freaked out. 'I'm sorry to say Mrs McDonald won't be back until after the Christmas holidays. But her replacement should be here any minute. He's had a long way to come.'

Rosie put her hand up. 'I already know who he is, don't I, Mr Noblet?'

'Yes, I suppose you do, Rosie,' said Mr Noblet.

'As well as owning the shopping centre in town, my daddy is a school governor,' explained Rosie to everyone (not that anybody actually cared). 'This means he's way more important than any of your parents . . .'

'Really?' said Vanya Goyal coolly. 'Because my dad's a doctor at a children's hospital and my mum's the top police officer in the whole city.'

Vanya Goyal is my other best friend, although she's a bit better than Gamble. In fact, she's the nicest, coolest girl in the class. She's also tough enough to stand up to Rosie. She hadn't been at the panto the night before because she'd had a karate competition.

'Huh,' said Rosie, holding up her palm to Vanya.

'Sick kids are totally gross. And who wants to be a police officer anyway? Black uniforms and fluorescent jackets? Yuck! Your mother should arrest *herself* for wearing frumptabulous clothes.'

'Wow,' I said.

Rosie carried on. 'As I was saying before I was rudely interrupted, my daddy is a school governor, so he's kind of like Mr Noblet's boss.'

'Well . . .' said Mr Noblet, who didn't look like he totally agreed with her.

'And,' said Rosie, ignoring him, 'he chose Mrs McDonald's replacement especially because this teacher is an **actual, proper actor** and he'll make our Christmas performance *utterly perfect*, won't he, Mr Noblet?'

'Yes, I hope so,' nodded Mr Noblet. 'And we've all got Rosie's dad to thank bec—'

'Because,' said Rosie over him, 'Mrs McDonald is completely useless at drama and acting, isn't she, Mr Noblet?'

'I wouldn't go that far . . .'

'Er . . . she is. Trust me. I know everything. So it was really great that Mrs McDonald broke her arm and got set on fire before she could ruin our play, wasn't it, Mr Noblet?'

Yikes! Rosie really is dreadful.

'I . . . well . . . er . . . no . . .' spluttered Mr Noblet.

'I mean,' continued Rosie, 'having a terrible teacher in charge of the play wouldn't affect *my* performance because I'm already world-class at acting, but imagine the damage it could do to all the talentless frugs like Roman.'

'*Frugs?*' I asked.

Rosie smiled. 'It's a mash-up of freaks and slugs. No offence.'

I looked up at the ceiling. 'None taken.'

'So anyway, my daddy stayed up all night to find a drama expert to take over the class. And he's paying him double wages out of his own pocket just to make me happy because I'm his little princess.'

'So who is this so-called *drama expert?*' Vanya asked, not sounding convinced.

'Well,' said Rosie, 'FYI, he's just been in a massive production. And he has loads of contacts in the showbiz world.'

'What's contacts?' asked Gamble, who'd stopped biting through the wire and was now licking the plug socket.

Rosie rolled her eyes. 'He told my daddy that he knows loads of people who work in film and TV, and he's going to put me in touch with them so that I can become a superstar.'

At that moment, the door swung open. Nobody appeared to be there. But then, after a few moments, the strangest-looking man I've ever seen appeared in the doorway and swept into the room.

Mr Le Gonk

Now I'm pretty stumpy, but this man was even smaller than me. He had a huge, perfectly round belly. His legs were short and skinny, with tiny feet that skimmed across the floor as he moved. He looked like a beach ball balancing on a couple of pins, which could burst it at any moment.

And if his body was weird, then his face was even worse. It was all squashed and stretched, as if it'd been made out of plasticine then attacked by a clumsy baby. He had beady eyes and a tiny, snubby nose, but his mouth was enormous, with lips like two flabby sausages. On top of all this, he had the biggest hair of all time – a humongous black tidal wave that rolled up from his forehead.

Nobody knew what to say.

'Charmed,' he said. His voice was deep and slow, like a barrel of hot jam being stirred with a trombone. 'Bartholomew J. Le Gonk, at your service.'

'*Le Gonk?*' whispered Vanya.

I giggled. *What a weird name.* It sounded like something a Belgian person might find between their toes.

Before Mr Noblet could say anything, Rosie leaped out of her chair and shook Mr Le Gonk's hand vigorously. 'On behalf of everyone, may I say welcome to our school? I can't wait to learn from an acting master such as yourself.'

'Ah. You must be Rosie,' he replied warmly. 'The daughter of the very *generous* man who hired me. Wonderful to meet you.'

Of course Mr Le Gonk would be nice to Rosie. Her *generous* dad was paying him double money to work here.

Over on the far side of the room, Gamble snorted something out of the back of his throat and spat behind the bookcase. 'You'll never be as good as Mrs McDonald.'

Mr Le Gonk looked at him and jumped backwards. 'Yikes! What a strange creature.'

'Just . . . don't go too near it,' said Rosie. 'You wouldn't want to catch bum worms.'

'Oi! I ain't got worms,' sniffed Gamble. 'That's my dog. And my uncle.'

'Ready to start, Mr Le Gonk?' asked Mr Noblet, hastily changing the subject.

'Ah yes,' Mr Le Gonk announced. 'I hear that we are in the midst of a dramatic emergency.'

'Er . . . well . . .' said Mr Noblet. Like the rest of us, I don't think he had the foggiest idea what Mr Le Gonk was on about.

'The gentleman on the phone informed me that we have but four days . . .' Mr Le Gonk paused and put a chubby knuckle into his mouth as if this news made him deeply upset. '**Four days** until . . . *la grande performance.*'

I think this last bit may have been French. Well, Mr Le Gonk said it with a French accent and waved his arms about. So it *seemed* French, even if it was actually just nonsense.

He smiled a huge, sausage-lipped smile. 'So, my darlings. Let us wait no longer. Onward to the performance space. Immediately!'

He clapped his hands three times, spun round on his tiny heels and scampered out of the room with his nose high in the air.

What a peculiar fellow, I thought to myself.

Mr Noblet seemed to think the same thing. 'Er . . . right . . . well . . . I suppose you should all go to the hall and . . . er . . . show him what you've been practising.'

Five Minutes Later . . .

We'd all done as we were told.

We'd all trooped into the hall and performed our song and dance onstage.

Our song was called 'The Brussels Sprout Boogie' – three minutes of wiggling our bodies and singing silly lines about swimming around in gravy and being left lonely on the plate.

Normally I hate being onstage. I don't like being the centre of attention. I get nervous and embarrassed easily. Still – I didn't mind doing this song too much. It was quite funny. And because the whole class was up there, I could hide behind the taller kids so that the audience wouldn't see me.

So, we'd followed every step, every movement

and every note, exactly as Mrs McDonald had taught us. And now we were standing there, waving our jazz hands and grinning for the big finale, exactly like we'd been told to do as well.

Mr Le Gonk was sitting on a chair in the middle of the room watching us. His face was blank, his body completely still.

We all carried on grinning and waving our jazz hands.

Ten seconds. Fifteen seconds.

Mr Le Gonk did not move.

His little legs were crossed and his fingers were interlocked under his chin.

Still grinning and waving, a few people began shuffling their feet.

Forty-five seconds. A minute.

This was getting ridiculous.

Eventually, the jazz hands slowed down, till we looked more like a bunch of C-3POs with low batteries.

The grins became more like chimpanzees suffering from bad wind.

And still he did not move.

Is he . . . dead? I thought, *Were we so good that we'd actually killed him?*

Eventually Mr Noblet broke the silence. He was standing next to Mr Le Gonk. 'So . . . er . . . what did you think?'

Mr Le Gonk smiled at him. 'My dear man. May I please have a few moments alone with my cast?'

'Oh . . . er . . . of course,' said Mr Noblet, giving us the thumbs up as he left the room.

When Mr Noblet had gone, Mr Le Gonk took a deep breath. 'That was . . .'

We all leaned forward to hear what this great actor was going to say. *Had he enjoyed it?*

'THE most . . .' He paused and took a deep breath, closing his eyes as if searching for the word.

'. . . amazing thing you've ever seen?' offered Rosie Taylor.

'*THE* most . . .' repeated Le Gonk, 'appalling pile of donkey droppings to have ever been plopped out onto a stage.'

'Oh,' I said.

The jazz hands stopped. The grins disappeared.

'It was an insult to the theatre,' ranted Mr Le Gonk, leaping to his feet. 'It was the worst thing I have ever seen in my career. And trust me, I have seen an actor eaten alive by an angry crowd.'

'Cool,' said Gamble.

'They left only his teeth,' said Mr Le Gonk sadly.

'That's horrible . . .' moaned Kevin *Vomasaurus Retch* Harrison, before bending over and throwing up noisily into the Christmas tree's plant pot.

Mr Le Gonk curled up his big sausage lips in disgust. 'True actors are never ill onstage. I once worked with Sir Boris McFluff, who performed for three hours after accidentally chopping off his entire lower leg. Now, kindly get off my stage, *Puke Skywalker.*'

Kevin trudged miserably out of the room.

Puke Skywalker!? I might actually have laughed if Mr Le Gonk hadn't been so angry. And if I hadn't been standing quite so close to the Christmas tree.

'Still,' said Le Gonk, waving a hand at the plant pot full of sick, 'I'd rather watch that boy emptying his stomach than have to sit through that so-called performance again.'

'Was there anything you *did* like about it?' Vanya Goyal asked Mr Le Gonk.

'Yes, darling,' said Mr Le Gonk, giving a fake smile which he then quite suddenly dropped. 'The bit when it stopped happening.'

A few people tittered.

'THAT WAS NOT MEANT TO BE AMUSING!' yelled Mr Le Gonk, his voice ringing out across the room.

A moment later, Mr Noblet popped his head around the door. 'Is everything OK? I heard shouting.'

Mr Le Gonk gave him a charming smile. 'Of course, my dear man,' he lied. 'Just telling these wonderful actors how good they were.'

'Excellent,' said Mr Noblet, ducking back out again.

As soon as he'd gone, Mr Le Gonk's smile dropped again. 'I should walk out of this door and never return. But instead . . .' He raised his finger. 'I will stay for the rest of the week.'

Everyone groaned but he didn't seem to notice. 'For, if I do not, you will let your audience down. And there is no greater crime than that!'

With that, he swept towards the door.

'What about murder?' asked Vanya. 'Isn't that a worse crime than letting down an audience?'

'Shut your trap, whoever said that,' said Mr Le Gonk without turning round. 'And follow me to the classroom, all of you. The hard work begins immediately!'

'I don't like Mr Le Gonk much,' said Vanya to me as we walked back behind him.

'Me neither,' I replied.

'Well,' said Rosie Taylor, appearing in between us, 'I think he's FANTASTIC!'

'You would,' I tutted.

'He's a *proper actor*,' she said. 'He's got high standards. Hopefully he'll kick all the grimbots like you out of the performance and just keep the talented ones. Like me. My very own one-woman show. Wouldn't that be fantastic? His friends from the TV and film industry would love it.'

I snorted. I'd been standing right behind Rosie during the performance, and she was awful. When she sings she sounds like a pig being beaten to death with an out-of-tune violin.

Rosie pursed her slug's bum mouth. 'I was the only thing he liked.'

'No,' said Vanya, 'he said he liked the bit when it stopped.'

'Exactly,' replied Rosie, 'and *I* stopped ten seconds before anyone else.'

With that she strutted off ahead of us.

I frowned. 'I'm not an expert,' I said to Vanya,

'but weren't we all meant to finish at the same time?'

Alone

When we arrived back in class, Mr Le Gonk announced, 'Forthwith, I must retire to my creative space and compose a new masterpiece.'

'Eh?' asked Vanya.

Mr Le Gonk sniffed. 'I'm going in here to write a new play cos your one is rubbish.'

And with that, he spun on his heel, opened the door of the storage cupboard, stepped inside and shut the door behind him.

'He *does* realise that he's in a cupboard, doesn't he?' I asked Vanya.

'Of course I do,' came Mr Le Gonk's muffled voice from behind the door. 'I need to be alone.'

'And what would you like us to do while you're sitting in the cupboard?' called out Vanya. 'We're meant to be having lessons.'

'Stop interrupting him, Vanya, you dreadful nappy head,' tutted Rosie Taylor. 'Mr Le Gonk is a creative genius. He's trying to write a play that makes the most of his star performer – AKA me.

How can he concentrate with you bothering him all the time?'

Vanya rolled her eyes. 'Oh, I'm so sorry for coming to school and wanting to learn something.'

Mr Le Gonk poked his ridiculous head out from around the door. 'If you're bored, I suggest you all sit in silence and think about how awful you were onstage. And when you've finished doing that, ask that weird-shaped woman over there for something else to do.'

He disappeared back inside the cupboard.

We all looked over at Miss Clegg, who was obviously the weird-shaped woman he was talking about. She'd logged onto the computer and appeared to be Skyping one of her friends. 'So,' she said to the woman on the screen (who looked pretty much like a clone of her), 'tell me more about your new boyfriend . . .'

It took her a while to realise we were all looking at her. She slowly turned her massive head round towards us. 'What?'

'You need to tell us what to do,' said Vanya.

'Oh,' she yawned, 'just . . . er . . . I don't know . . . do something. Or something like that.'

Miss Clegg isn't exactly an inspirational teacher.

'Thank you so much,' said Vanya.

Miss Clegg didn't notice her sarcasm. She'd already gone back to her Skype call. 'Nothing,' she said to her clone-friend. 'Anyway. Back to more important stuff – this man. Has he got any handsome friends . . . ?'

Rule one of teaching: it's a bad idea to tell a roomful of kids to 'just do something', then let them get on with it.

Especially when one of those kids is Darren Gamble.

Within minutes the whole place was total chaos. People were shouting and running around and throwing things at each other. Rosie had taken out her mobile phone and was uploading videos to the internet of herself murdering a range of pop songs.

Darren Gamble had tied Kevin *Puke Skywalker* Harrison to Mrs McDonald's desk, and was leaning over his neck with a pair of sharp scissors.

'HELP!' yelled Kevin. 'I'm going to hurl.'

'Stop being a wuss and keep still,' said Gamble. 'You won't feel a thing. One flick of the scissors and I'll have your head clean off.'

'But I like my head!' wailed Kevin.

Gamble tutted. 'Don't be soft. I'll sellotape on something really cool in its place. Like a lightbulb. Or a bog roll. Or a pigeon's foot or summat.'

Kevin passed out.

'That's better,' said Gamble. 'I won't need to use that anaesthetic I stole from the hospital now.'

Luckily for Kevin, at that moment the classroom door flew open. 'What's going on?' asked Mr Noblet.

Fire Safety

Apart from Kevin, everyone scurried back to their places and sat quietly. Even Miss Clegg huffed out her cheeks and hung up on her Skype call.

Mr Noblet was holding an iPad in his hand. He looked around the room. 'Where is Mr Le Gonk?'

At that moment, Mr Le Gonk opened the cupboard and burst out. 'It is I – Le Gonk!'

'He's writing a play in the cupboard, Mr Noblet,' Vanya said.

'Oh,' said Mr Noblet.

'And how may I be of assistance?' asked Mr Le Gonk. I'd noticed he was an awful lot nicer whenever Mr Noblet was in the room.

'Well,' said Mr Noblet, 'after what happened to Mrs McDonald, I must look into fire safety in the school . . .'

Mr Le Gonk narrowed his eyes. 'Fire safety?'

'Yes,' said Mr Noblet, 'it's extremely important. Are we doing enough to stay safe from fire? We cannot afford any more accidents. I have a company coming in tomorrow to see how well-prepared for a fire the school is. Before then, I want to ask these guys what they think.'

Mr Noblet is one of those *cool* teachers who always calls us things like 'guys' and tells us that what we think is really important.

At that moment, a phone rang. It was coming from Miss Clegg's computer.

'Oh great,' she moaned. 'Mrs McDonald. I thought we'd got rid of her.'

Gamble nipped in front of her and clicked the mouse to answer the Skype call. Mrs McDonald appeared on the screen. She seemed to be in a hospital bed, surrounded by flowers and enormous fluffy guinea-pig toys.

'Darren!' said Mrs McDonald. 'What a nice surprise.'

I don't think that these words had ever been said before.

'How are you, miss?' said Gamble, hugging the monitor.

'Much better, thank you. The burns weren't as bad as first thought. No real damage, apart from the broken arm. I'll be out tomorrow and back at work after Christmas.'

'I've missed you, miss. If you want, I can go and find that Madame Boom Boom and I can beat her up or I can just get some papier-mâché and use it to turn her car into a giant willy or something, miss.'

Mrs McDonald held up her hand with the plaster cast on it. 'Oh, that won't be necessary, Darren. I noticed that Miss Clegg was online and thought I'd say hello. I've just been video-calling my guinea pigs.'

Video-calling her guinea pigs?

I glanced at Vanya.

'Probably best not to ask,' she muttered. Mrs McDonald is completely obsessed with her pet guinea pigs.

'And how are you all?' continued Mrs McDonald.

'We've got a new teacher, miss, and he's a right fat-headed bog-scrubber.'

'Well, that's not nice, Darren,' said Mrs McDonald. 'You must do as your new teacher says.'

Gamble saluted her earnestly. 'OK, miss. I'll do whatever he tells me to, miss. Anything for you, miss.'

Mr Le Gonk strode forward and shoved Gamble out of the way. 'Am I right in thinking that you are responsible for the children's song and dance?'

Mrs McDonald smiled. 'Yes. Have they been practising? I think it's rather good. Hopefully I'll be able to come and watch on Frid—'

Mr Le Gonk yanked the computer wire out of the wall. The screen went black. Gamble grabbed hold of the screen and looked behind it, then shook it as if he was expecting Mrs McDonald to fall out.

'Whoops,' said Mr Le Gonk.

'What did you do that for, cheese-face,' he snapped, swinging round to face Mr Le Gonk and forgetting his promise to Mrs McDonald.

'We must cut our ties with the past,' said Mr Le Gonk, raising a finger. 'From now on we look to the future.'

'Hear hear,' said Rosie.

'Carry on as you were, class,' said Mr Le Gonk, darting back towards the cupboard.

'Where are you going?' said Mr Noblet. 'I wanted you to help me talk to the children about fire safety. It's important.'

Mr Le Gonk smiled kindly at him. 'My dear fellow. I'm writing a play. There's nothing more important than that.'

There was a long silence.

'Isn't fire safety more important than a play?' asked Vanya.

'No, it is not!' snapped Mr Le Gonk, a flash of irritation appearing on his face. 'There is nothing in the world more important than writing a play.'

'Exactly,' said Rosie Taylor, shaking her head at Vanya.

I'm pretty sure Mr Le Gonk was wrong about this. There are loads of things that are more important than writing a play: fire safety, doughnuts, hospitals, schools, more doughnuts, the police, other types of doughnuts. The list goes on (with most of the things on it being doughnuts).

'But you're meant to be teach–' began Mr Noblet.

Mr Le Gonk smiled and clapped him round the

shoulder. 'I'm sure you're more than capable of taking over. Good man.'

With that, he disappeared back into his cupboard and shut the door.

Mr Noblet stood there for a while, looking confused. It was like he didn't know how to deal with Mr Le Gonk at all. There was something about the way Mr Le Gonk spoke in that rich, deep voice that made you do as he told you, even if you knew it was stupid.

Eventually, Mr Noblet cleared his throat and stroked his moustache. 'Well. Er. OK. While I'm here, do any of *you* have any ideas about fire safety?'

'Everyone should spray their clothes with petrol when they come into school, sir,' said Gamble.

I slapped my hand against my forehead.

'Er . . . but petrol is *highly flammable*,' said Mr Noblet, his moustache bristling uneasily. 'One tiny spark and the whole lot of you would go up in flames. That would be the most dangerous thing we could possibly do.'

'Think about it though,' said Gamble. 'We'd all be a lot more careful round fires if we thought we could blow up if we went near one.'

I suppose this did make some sense. In a Gamble kind of way.

'Plus I've always dreamed of being a human fireball,' he continued.

Mr Noblet didn't seem to know what to say to this.

'How about sprinklers?' I said. 'You know – those things in the ceiling that spray water out if there's a fire.'

At that, Mr Noblet's face lit up. 'By crikey! That's a great idea. We'll look into it! Good work, Norman.'

'Roman,' I said flatly. I wasn't *that* annoyed though. I mean, this was the first time in seven years at the school that I'd ever come up with a good idea. I felt myself blushing.

Little did I know that, by the end of the week, this would turn out to be the worst idea I had ever had. In fact, it was the worst idea that *anybody* had ever had. It was an idea that would cause absolute misery to everyone in the school.

'I still think soaking ourselves in petrol was better,' grumbled Gamble.

The way things turned out, he was probably right.

You see, that sweaty little mince pie that Gamble had brought to the panto had already caused some huge changes:

Mince pie swapped
with Fruit Pastilles.

Mrs McDonald
gets set on fire.

Mr Noblet
becomes obsessed
with fire safety.

We get a weird new teacher
who changes our play.

But this was just the start of it.

Things were about to become a lot more serious. Those evil pies were about to take over our lives.

TUESDAY

Morning

We Go Inside Mr Le Gonk's Mind and Find Out Just How Weird It Is in There

The rest of Monday had been really strange. Mr Le Gonk hadn't emerged from the cupboard at all. A couple of times, Mr Noblet had tried the door, but there was no answer. He must've somehow locked it from inside.

After a while, Mr Noblet gave up and just stayed in with us. We spent most of the afternoon doing work on fire safety before going home at three o'clock.

The next morning, we arrived to an empty classroom. We were just wondering what was going on when the cupboard door creaked open, and there stood Mr Le Gonk.

He didn't look good. He was wearing the same clothes as yesterday, which were now crumpled and creased. His enormous hair had sort of flopped to the side, like a hot air balloon with a puncture, and there were black streaks running across his face from his eyes. A thick stack of paper was clutched in his podgy hands.

Seeming surprised to see us, he blinked against the light. 'Why are you still here? Should've gone home hours ago. What time is it?'

'Tuesday,' I said, realising that this wasn't really a time.

Mr Le Gonk's eyes nearly popped out of his head. 'Tuesday!? But . . . that means . . .'

'Hang on,' said Vanya after a moment. 'Did you *sleep* in the cupboard?'

Mr Le Gonk went bright red. Then he regained himself, pulling his trousers up over his huge belly and puffing out his chest. 'What a ridiculous suggestion. How dare you?'

'Well, you've not got changed. And your make-up is all smudged across your face, like you've been asleep with your head resting on your arm.'

Make-up. Ah – so <u>that's</u> what the black smudges were.

A few people giggled and muttered, 'Mr Le Gonk wears make-up,' to each other.

'W-well . . .' spluttered Mr Le Gonk, 'of course one wears make-up at all times. When one is an actor, one must always be ready to perform. One never knows when one might have to leap onto a stage in an emergency and perform in a play. Someone's life could depend on it.'

Unlikely . . . I thought.

'And anyway,' he continued, strutting over to the teacher's chair and sitting down, his little feet dangling above the floor, 'I did *not* stay here overnight.'

'Course not,' said Vanya.

Mr Le Gonk ignored her. 'I merely arrived early this morning to finish your play. And finish it I did!'

He brandished the pile of paper in the air.

A few people went, '*Oooooooh.*'

My heart sank. I didn't want to practise a new play. It'd been hard enough learning how to be a Brussels sprout. I couldn't imagine how difficult Mr Le Gonk's play was going to be.

And secondly, I never trust people who sleep in

cupboards. Like that time Gamble came round to my house then disappeared. I found him at eleven o'clock that night, dangling upside down from the clothes rail in my wardrobe like a bat. I asked him what he was doing and he said he was waiting till I fell asleep so he could turn into a vampire and drink my blood.

'Oh, how *wonderful*!' gushed Rosie Taylor. 'Finally, someone with real talent is taking charge. I can't *wait* to act it out. Will you be inviting your friends who work in film and TV to watch us?'

Mr Le Gonk rubbed his eyes like he wasn't sure what she was on about. Then he shook himself and smiled at her. 'Of course, my dear. Of course.'

'*Hashtag*: eeek! Can't wait. Three cheers for Mr Le Gonk.'

He raised an imaginary hat to Rosie, but nobody joined in the cheers.

'Ignore these scummy peasants, Mr Le Gonk,' snapped Rosie. 'They wouldn't know a good play if it bit them on the brain.'

'*Can* a play bite you?' I murmured to Vanya. 'I mean, technically, it doesn't have a mouth, or teeth.'

'Enough!' roared Mr Le Gonk. 'The script is

complete. But now the work must begin. To the theatre!'

'I think he means the hall,' said Vanya.

When we got there, Mr Le Gonk made us all sit on the floor while he stood in front of us on the stage. 'I will now introduce you to my masterpiece.'

'You what?' mumbled Gamble, from over by the Christmas tree. It was hard to understand him because he had a bunch of fairy lights stuffed into his mouth.

'Gadzooks, what a fool,' muttered Mr Le Gonk, pinching his nose. 'I *mean*, I will show you my play. Prepare to journey through my mind.'

Mr Le Gonk's Mind

It turned out that Mr Le Gonk's mind was a very, very odd place to take a journey through. What followed was the weirdest twenty minutes of my life.

Before he started, he told us that the play was called *Inside the Mince Pie*. It was a 'challenging and daring piece of experimental theatre, music and dance that would push back the boundaries of imagination.'

Nope – I didn't have a clue what he was on about either.

But, helpfully, he acted the play out for us himself. This meant that we could figure out what he meant for ourselves. We figured out that 'challenging and daring' is a posh way of saying 'confusing and rubbish', and 'experimental theatre' just means 'a play that nobody understands'.

Oh, and 'pushing back the boundaries of imagination' is another way of saying 'completely nuts'.

Before I explain what we saw, you have to understand a few things:

1) When Mr Le Gonk acted out the play, he played ALL of the parts himself, even though there were at least thirty characters (if you count all the raisins. Yes, you read that correctly, the *raisins*).
2) This meant that sometimes he would have to have a conversation with himself, leaping from side to side so that he could play different people (in one scene he seemed to be playing eight characters, all with different voices).
3) Describing the play is impossible – it's like describing air, or explaining why doughnuts are so

tasty. As a result, I've just copied out a bit of Mr Le Gonk's actual script below. I promise I've not made any of it up.

4) When you read it, you might think it makes no sense. There's a good reason for this: **it's because it made no sense in real life either.**

Here goes:

Inside the Mince Pie
A Play
By Bartholomew J. Le Gonk,
PPA (Proper Professional Actor)

<u>Scene 1</u>
Lights are switched off. Room is in total darkness.

Strange Voice: [*coming from somewhere*]
                   Imagine a world of pastry.
                   Of mincemeat. Of DEATH.

Lights come on. The entire room, including the audience, is underneath a giant cream-coloured sheet (which represents the pastry).

The sheet hangs just above everybody's heads, giving the audience the impression of being trapped in a giant pie. The stage is ankle deep in a thick, sloppy liquid.[1]

Raisin King: I am the Raisin King. Worship me!

Other raisins bow down in the sludge.

Raisins: [*together*] Hail the Raisin King.

Raisin 1:   You're kneeling on my hand.

Raisin 2:   You don't have a hand. You're a raisin.

Raisin 1:   Oh yes. You're right.

Raisin King: We, the raisins of the mince pie, must escape from the land of pastry before it is eaten.

Raisins: [*Together*] Yes, Your Majesty.

---

1 The stage wasn't like this at the time, but Mr Le Gonk explained how he wanted it to look on the day.

SONG AND DANCE:
RAISIN' UP THE RAISINS [words and music by Bartholomew J. Le Gonk]

As the raisin actors sing, ten million actual raisins rain down onto the stage from above. The raisin actors use these to build a wall, using the sludge as mortar to stick them together. The wall must be ten feet high by the end of the song, and strong enough for all of the raisins to climb on top of.[2] *The raisins finish the song by trying to break through the sheet of pastry above their heads.*

Raisin King:	*[Looking up, scared]* Oh no! We're being attacked by the tooth army. Quickly. Run away!
Raisin 3:	We can't! We don't have legs!

---

2 I don't think Mr Le Gonk had thought this through. How were we supposed to build a wall out of raisins for heaven's sake?! It'd take years! Especially since he'd just said that the raisins who were building the wall didn't have arms.

The raisins are gripped with panic.[3]
Gigantic mechanical teeth burst through
the sheet, knocking down the wall and
grinding up the raisins (and possibly some
members of the audience). Note: to make
this realistic, some actors/audience
members may have to be actually injured
during this scene.[4]

You won't believe it, but that was the most normal
bit. After that, the play got *seriously* strange. I'll
try to explain what happened next, even though
I'm not entirely sure myself. I mean, I *think* this is
what I saw, but it's very possible that I fell asleep
and had the craziest dream of my entire life.

1) The mince pie is chewed up and eaten. The raisins
   end up in someone's stomach, along with the
   pastry and the sludge.
2) It turns out that they are in Santa Claus's stomach
   (DEN DEN DERRRRR!!), which they find out from

---

3 This is the only time in history that this sentence has ever
been written.

4 The script actually says this.

a wise old chunk of reindeer meat (I know – *I* didn't think Santa would eat reindeer meat either).

3) They want to leave but there is no way out unless they can get back up out of Santa's throat (well, I guess there would've been another way out but it's probably not a good idea to think too much about this).

4) They rebuild the mince pie from all the chewed-up sludge and crumbs of pastry. The piece of reindeer meat sprinkles magic dust on them and turns the mince pie into a flying saucer.

5) As they try to escape, they accidentally fly out through a magic portal in Santa's belly button (stick with it – it gets even more weird after this).

6) The portal leads them to the land of a magical evil queen who has built the magic portal so that she can get inside Santa's body and turn him evil. If the raisins don't stop her, nobody will get any presents and Christmas will be ruined.

Honestly. I am not making this up.

We all sat there, open-mouthed, gawping at this incredible spectacle. Only Rosie seemed to enjoy it. She had her hands clasped together and was weeping – seriously, *weeping* – and she kept saying things like 'Oh, how brave!' and '*Hashtag: wondertastical.*'

I have no idea what happened next in the play because, just as Mr Le Gonk was about to head through the magical portal and take on the evil queen, Mr Noblet came into the room, along with a woman I'd never seen before.

How Can You Sleep at Night?

Mr Le Gonk didn't notice them at first, and he carried on zooming around the stage in his imaginary mince pie flying saucer, making *peeew-peeew* noises. The woman and Mr Noblet stared at him, their eyes bulging out of their heads.

'Oh . . . er . . . is everything OK?' Mr Noblet asked.

Mr Le Gonk stopped.

'Mr Le Gonk was pretending to be a chewed-up-and-re-built mince pie flying saucer,' I said, realising straight away how ludicrous this sounded.

Mr Noblet's mouth made an 'O' shape.

'He was about to fly through a magic portal in Santa's belly button so they could save Christmas,' offered Vanya.

'I've swallowed a fairy light,' said Gamble. Amazingly, this was the most sensible thing anyone had said for at least twenty minutes.

'The play was magnificent,' gushed Rosie. 'A real treat to see a maestro at work.'

'Thank you,' smiled Mr Le Gonk. 'I know.'

'Well, don't mind us,' said Mr Noblet, sounding more confused than ever. 'Do carry on, Mr Le Gonk.'

'There is no point,' said Mr Le Gonk, dramatically flinging his hand to his forehead. 'The moment has gone.'

'Oh. Sorry ab—'

Mr Le Gonk stopped him with a raised finger. 'But, since you're here, I will require a small sum of money from the school to build my set and make it look like a pie. And a stomach. And a magical kingdom. Oh, and Mars.'

'MARS?' I blurted out.

'We haven't go to that bit in the play yet,' sniffed Mr Le Gonk. 'It's where they go to after we find out that the evil queen is actually an alien that hatched from an egg that Santa gave to the Emperor of Mars on Christmas Day two million years ago.'

Of course. Makes perfect sense . . .

Mr Noblet narrowed his eyes at Mr Le Gonk. 'What do you mean, a *small* sum of money?'

'Well . . . let me see,' muttered Mr Le Gonk. 'I'll need materials . . . mechanical teeth . . . carpenters . . . electricians . . . a flying saucer . . . special effects . . . lasers . . . ten million raisins . . .' He was looking upwards, as if trying to find the answer under his massive hair. 'I'd say . . . ooh . . . around about two hundred thousand pounds.'

Mr Noblet's moustache nearly flew off. '**Two hundred thousand pounds?!**'

'Maybe three hundred thousand just to be safe,' said Mr Le Gonk. 'I think you'll find it'll be worth it.'

'We can't afford that kind of money!' said Mr Noblet.

Mr Le Gonk looked horrified. 'But . . . but . . . how do you expect me to make this performance perfect?'

Mr Noblet jerked his thumb towards the woman next to him. 'Well, I'm sorry, but we're spending everything we've got on sprinklers to keep the children safe from fire.'

My suggestion was happening! I felt a little burst of pride.

The woman next to him smiled. 'My company will be fitting them tomorrow,' she said. 'I'm afraid the hall will be out of action for a few days.'

This news seemed to hit Mr Le Gonk pretty hard. He grabbed his heart and staggered backwards. 'So,' he gasped dramatically, 'not only are you stealing the money that should be paying for my play. You're also going to steal the rehearsal space. We won't be able to practise.'

'I know you're upset and I'm sorry. But we need these sprinklers fitted right away,' said Mr Noblet. 'You can't put off fire safety.'

'How do you sleep at night?' said Mr Le Gonk, shaking his head at the woman.

She frowned. 'Er. Quite well, actually. My sprinklers put out fires and save lives.'

'But what's the point of being alive if you can't enjoy a great play?' snarled Mr Le Gonk.

The woman didn't know what to say to this.

'Er, Mr Le Gonk,' piped up Rosie Taylor, '*status update* – just to remind you that the sprinklers were Roman's idea. So if you need someone to blame or you want to get your revenge, he's the perfect person.'

Thanks a bunch.

Mr Le Gonk glared at me. 'I will not forget this.'
I gulped.

Mr Noblet walked towards him. 'I'm really sorry,
Mr Le Gonk. But this is a school and w—'

'Fear not,' said Mr Le Gonk, a big false sausage-
lipped smile spreading across his face. 'Bartholomew
J. Le Gonk has dealt with far worse in his acting
career.' Then he raised a finger in the air and spun
towards the door. 'To the classroom. At once.'

Fundraising

Back in the classroom, Mr Le Gonk began writing
on the whiteboard. 'We have two problems,' he
said over his shoulder as he scribbled. Then he
stood back to reveal what he'd written:

1) **Nowhere to rehearse, thanks to the stupid,
   pointless sprinkler system.**
2) **Not enough money to pay for the set/special
   effects (see above).**

'Number one is bad enough but, with an expert like
yours truly to guide you, you should be able to
rehearse anywhere,' he said. 'I remember doing a

play in Australia with Dame Sharon Snuff. Our theatre was infested with duck-billed platypuses, so fourteen of us rehearsed in the back of a Ford Focus.'

I glanced at Vanya, who rolled her eyes. It seemed as if Mr Le Gonk had an endless supply of acting stories that were all complete and utter rubbish. *Duck-billed platypuses,* for heaven's sake.

'But number two is a bit more serious,' said Mr Le Gonk, striding back and forth with his hands behind his back. 'We need money fast.'

'We could rob it off people,' said Gamble. 'Or I could sell my undies.'

'Who'd buy *them*?' yawned Miss Clegg. 'Unless they were going to use them as a chemical weapon.'

Mr Le Gonk stopped and faced the class. 'No. We're going to have a fundraiser. Tomorrow. Right here in school. A Christmas market. Everything we raise will go towards paying for our play. Get in groups. Let's get planning!'

Gamble immediately leaped on me and said, 'I'm with you, Roman, cos I love you and you're my best friend.'

'Oh, that's nice,' I croaked.

'And if you work with anyone else I'll pull out your tongue and staple it to your forehead.'

'Right. That's settled then.'

In the other groups, there were loads of different ideas. Rosie was going to sell signed photos of herself (like anyone was going to buy *them*!). Vanya and a couple of other people would make and sell bead necklaces. Kevin *Puke Skywalker* Harrison was running a stall where you had to see how fast you could drink a large glass of banana milkshake while jumping up and down on a mini-trampoline.

'We're doing Santa's Grotto,' said Gamble before I could suggest anything else. 'You can be Santa. I'll be a cute little elf.'

'Cute?' snorted Miss Clegg. 'You're about as cute as a barrel of fish heads.'

She had a point.

'Shut your pie hole, you great dirty turtle's boob,' snapped Gamble, before turning back to me. 'I'll get my uncle Terry to lend us a caravan to use as the grotto. It'll be well good. The kids can pay a quid to get in. You'll give 'em a prezzie. Then I'll beat 'em up on the way out, and nick the prezzie back and anything else they've got in their pockets.'

'We can't do that,' I said wearily.

Gamble tutted. 'Can't do anything round here.'

'Anyway, I don't have a Santa outfit,' I said, 'and

we don't have any presents to give people in the first place.'

'Leave that to me,' replied Gamble, a mischievous grin on his face.

I gulped.

Afternoon

We Learn Just How Terrible
We All Are and How Worthless I Am

The rest of the morning was spent planning our stalls (not that Gamble told me anything about what we were doing), and making posters to stick up around the local area. I didn't really like our poster: Gamble insisted on me writing 'COME TO OUR CHRISTMAS FAIR OR WE'LL EAT YOUR BRAIN' on it.

After lunch (vegetable pie – seriously, *vegetables* – were they trying to kill us or something?), we had our first rehearsal of *Inside the Mince Pie*.

Before the rehearsal, Mr Le Gonk told all of us what parts we'd be playing. Rosie was given the part of the Evil Queen. I have to say that she was the perfect choice. She's the most evil person I've ever met.

'How should I act, Mr Le Gonk?' she asked. 'Should I be moody and mysterious, like Thelma Snutt in *What's That in My Sock*? Or should I be all-action and dangerous, like Tasmin Earthquake in *Attack of the Ninja Zombie Cucumbers*?'

Mr Le Gonk thought about this for a moment, his eyes closed. Then he raised a chubby finger in the air. 'The secret of great acting is this: do not **try** to be *anything*. You must **become** your character.'

'Great advice as always,' she simpered. 'You really are a genius, Mr Le Gonk. With your tips, I'm sure that your friends from the TV and film industry will love me on Friday.'

'Naturally,' said Mr Le Gonk.

I wasn't sure how I was going to **become** my character. I was playing a chewed-up pea inside Santa's stomach, and I didn't actually have any lines. Mr Le Gonk told me that I was there to 'show how disgusting the inside of a stomach is', and I should just 'slop about, looking grim'.

'In other words, just be yourself,' smiled Rosie. I got the feeling that she might have put him up to it.

Vanya was going to be the Emperor of Mars, Gamble was the Evil Queen's monkey-butler, and Kevin *Puke Skywalker Harrison* was the Raisin King. Seriously – Kevin had a better part than me! I mean, don't get me wrong, I didn't *want* a big role in the play, but still – the only other time Kevin had been onstage this week, he'd thrown up on a Christmas tree.

After we'd been given our parts, we followed Mr Le Gonk to the hall (or 'rehearsal space' as he called it).

Foundation Stage

When we arrived in the hall, the Foundation Stage kids were on the stage practising their song (entitled 'Wiggling Wise Men') for the performance. Their teacher, Miss Pickles, was kneeling on the floor in front of the stage, miming the actions for them to copy.

We all filed in quietly and watched. Everyone loves it when the little kids go onstage. They always look a bit surprised to be there. Only about half of them were singing and dancing. Some were randomly spinning around, others were staring into space or playing bumper cars. One had even taken her shoe off and was sitting on the floor, chewing it.

Even so, they did look seriously cute.

Mr Le Gonk didn't seem to think so though. He looked like he'd just trodden in something quite revolting.

When they'd finished, Miss Pickles stood up and turned to smile at him. She's really nice, like a warm cuddle on legs. 'Oh, hello,' she sang. Her voice is all floaty and babyish from speaking to little children all day. 'You must be Mrs McDonald's weplacement. Such a shame when she got a teeny-weeny bit set on fire.'

'Quite,' said Mr Le Gonk, putting on a fat, fake, sausagey smile back. His voice was friendly enough but you could tell he was annoyed. 'May I enquire as to what you are doing?'

Miss Pickles wrinkled her nose at him. 'Well, we thought we'd sneak in here and have an inky-dinky lickle pwactice, didn't we, childwen?'

'Yes, Miss Pickles,' said some of her class, while picking their noses and rearranging their underpants.

'But, my dear lady, the hall is closed as of tomorrow, so they can fit a *sprinkler system*.' He made *sprinkler system* sound like *poo cannon*. 'I require it this afternoon so I can practise my masterpiece.'

'Yes,' said Miss Pickles. 'Miss Pickles saw how you had cwossed out Miss Pickles's names on the timetable and witten your own name instead. And Miss Pickles thought that was vewy cwever of you, but we didn't think you'd get all gwumpy gum gums if we wehearsed our song for a minny-winny before you started your pwactice, did we, childwen?' Her voice had got even more babyish, and her head was nodding like a woodpecker.

'Yes, Miss Pickles.'

Mr Le Gonk raised one eyebrow at Miss Pickles. 'How . . . *enchanting*.'

Miss Pickles didn't seem to notice how sarcastic he was being. She's one of those super-nice people who find it hard to believe that anyone could ever be horrible.

'Now sit up stwaight, childwen,' she said. 'This nice man is a vewy good actor. Maybe he'll tell you what he liked best of all about your pwactice.'

'Oh, I couldn't tell you what I liked best . . .' said Mr Le Gonk.

'Oh, pwetty pwease,' said Miss Pickles, wrinkling up her face.

'No, I mean I *honestly* couldn't tell you what I liked about it,' said Mr Le Gonk. 'Because the whole thing was soooooo . . . you know –' he swallowed hard – '. . . *bad.*'

For a few moments there was total silence in the room.

What?

I looked around. *He hadn't just said that, had he?*

'I'm s-sowwy?' asked Miss Pickles, gulping like a stranded fish.

'No . . . not *bad* . . .' said Mr Le Gonk. 'It was more . . . well . . . you know . . .' He waved his arm around for a few moments then huffed out his cheeks. 'Actually, no, I was right the first time. It was *bad.* Really, really bad.'

Yep. He had *said it, all right.*

'But . . . but they're four years old,' spluttered Miss Pickles.

Mr Le Gonk grinned at her. 'Yes. And they're very cute. But we need to face facts. They're just not cut out for life on the stage, darling. I mean, the singing was flat, most of them didn't know the dance steps. And this young fellow was picking his . . . *ahem* . . . bum the whole way through.'

A young boy looked up, his hand still down the back of his trousers.

'I mean,' he continued, trying to sound as kind as possible, 'imagine I'd done that during my latest production. I'd have been kicked out of the building. Why not leave it to the professionals in future?'

Miss Pickles tried to say something, but all she could do was make a bunch of incomprehensible noises.

Mr Le Gonk patted her on the head. Seriously, the *head*, like she was some kind of sick puppy. 'Don't let this put you off though, darling. *Do* try again next year. And *do* have a lovely day.'

Amazingly, he said this as though he was actually being nice to her.

The Foundation Stage kids all trudged out, with Miss Pickles looking back at Mr Le Gonk the whole time. Her face was hot pink and her mouth was hanging open.

Nobody could speak. Except for Rosie Taylor, that is. 'Bravo, Mr Le Gonk!' she simpered. 'I think it's wonderful that you set such high standards. Otherwise any old rubbish could get onto the stage.'

For some reason, she seemed to be looking at me when she said this.

Mr Le Gonk seemed completely unaware of how rude he'd just been.

'The theatre is a place for honesty,' he said gravely. 'Sometimes, honesty is the most painful thing.'

We'd find out quite how painful honesty could be that afternoon.

The First Rehearsal

The first rehearsal went really well.

If by 'really well' I mean that, afterwards, Mr Le Gonk called us 'the most useless bunch of slugs to ever slither onto a stage', and that twenty-three people ended up crying.

The practice went on all afternoon. This was because Mr Le Gonk turned into the world's nastiest person as soon as we started. Every three seconds he would stop to scream at someone: 'You're meant to be a lump of reindeer flesh. You look more like a wet chicken nugget!' Or, 'Is that the most raisiny voice you can do?' Or (most often), 'Why can't you just be more like **ME**?'

He even yelled at me: 'You're meant to be a half-eaten pea. You look nowhere near chewed-up enough'.

I had no idea what he was on about by the way. How on earth was I supposed to look more chewed-up? Rosie suggested that I should nail bacon to my face and 'go and find some hungry homeless people'.

She really is a terrible human being.

In fact, Rosie was the only person he didn't scream at. I don't think that this was because she was any good at acting. I thought she was completely useless. Obviously, she got the whole *being evil* thing absolutely perfect, but she put on this weird croaky voice that made her sound like she had a live toad up her nose. Plus, she kept doing things that weren't in the script. Like repeatedly kicking me off the stage for instance.

Obviously, there were two good reasons why Mr Le Gonk didn't shout at Rosie:

1) The fact her dad was paying him double money.
2) She spent half her time telling him how brilliant he was. 'You're a *genius*, Mr Le Gonk,' and, 'Thank you so much for writing this line, Mr Le Gonk – it's *such* a privilege to be able to say it out loud,' and, 'Please show me again how an acting virtuoso like you would walk across the stage.'

Yuk!

All her gushing made me feel like Kevin *Puke Skywalker* Harrison that time when he ate a whole box of strawberry bootlaces then got stuck up a tree.

In fact, the only decent moment of the afternoon was when the fire alarm suddenly went off.

'Typical!' snapped Mr Le Gonk. 'Right! Everybody out. Most talented actors to the front. We need to save them first.'

I was just shuffling out of the door at the back of the line when I felt a tap on my shoulder.

It was Mr Noblet, the head teacher. He put a finger over his lips so I would keep quiet. As everybody else trotted outside onto the cold field, he led me back to his office, giggling.

'Sit down, relax,' he said when we got there. 'Have a marshmallow.'

There were a few other kids in there from different classes, all sitting on beanbags and happily munching sweets. It was incredible: I had joined a secret marshmallow club, while everyone else in the school was outside, shivering. This was the best thing that'd happened to anyone ever.

Mr Noblet had a mischievous glint in his eye.

'It's a little trick – a fire safety test. All of the teachers will be missing one child when they get out onto the field. I want to see what they do about it.'

I wasn't really listening to him though. By the time he'd finished speaking I was already buried face first in a bowl of Flumps.

We stayed there for five minutes. Then I found out exactly how worthless I really am.

Absolutely Nothing

Mr Noblet had a great big satisfied grin on his face as he led us out onto the field afterwards.

The rest of the kids in the school were in their lines, noses blue and teeth chattering. Our class wasn't though. They were spread out across part of the field, still practising the play.

Most of the teachers looked seriously relieved to see their missing children.

'Well done, everyone!' bellowed Mr Noblet. 'Fire safety is the most important thing in our school.'

'Apart from the play, of course,' called out Rosie Taylor.

Mr Le Gonk nodded his head. 'Exactly.'

Mr Noblet didn't seem to hear them. 'Now. Teachers. You may notice I stole a child from each of you. What did you do about it?'

It turned out that most of the teachers had done quite a lot about it. Two of them had run back into the school to search for missing children ('Brave but dangerous. Leave it to the fire brigade in future,' said Mr Noblet); others had triple-checked their registers, sent teaching assistants to look round the outside of the building, and collected names of missing children for when the fire fighters arrived ('Perfect response,' said Mr Noblet).

And then there was Mr Le Gonk.

He had found out I was missing and he had done nothing.

Absolutely nothing.

He'd just continued to practise his play and hadn't given me a second thought.

'Why didn't you do anything?' asked Mr Noblet, surprised.

Mr Le Gonk hoisted his trousers over his fat belly and sniffed. 'We didn't really need him in this scene.'

Thanks a lot.

'But what if he'd been trapped in the school?'

'Ooh yes!' grinned Rosie, clapping her hands together. 'Sounds great!'

Mr Le Gonk shrugged. 'I could've changed the script, I suppose, and got rid of the chewed-up pea.'

I felt a little bit faint.

'But . . . but . . .' said Mr Noblet, 'Rogan is a *child*.'

'Roman,' I said flatly.

'Oh gosh!' exclaimed Mr Le Gonk, putting his hand over his mouth. 'I see! You mean, what if the poor little chap had been caught up in a fire?'

'Getting better by the second,' said Rosie.

'Well, that would've been tragic, my dear man, simply *tragic*,' said Mr Le Gonk. He took a deep breath, and a single tear dribbled down his cheek. He was very good at pretending to care.

Mr Noblet looked like he believed him though. 'Yes. What would you have done, then?'

'Hmmm,' sighed Mr Le Gonk, 'I suppose I could've performed a one-man show at his funeral. Something light. A few jokes. Maybe a happy song? Cheer everyone up a bit.'

I gulped.

'Oh,' said Mr Noblet, 'that wasn't quite wh—'

'Fabulous to chat to you, darling' said Mr Le

Gonk, clapping him on the back. 'But we must go inside. The cold weather can really damage an actor's throat. Toodle-oo. We'll do lunch together tomorrow.'

Stuff to Do, Innit

Of course, the moment Mr Noblet was out of sight, Mr Le Gonk went back to being horrible again. The rest of the afternoon was pretty much the same as what had gone before. In other words, we acted out Mr Le Gonk's crazy play while he found new ways of telling us how rubbish we were.

We were fifteen minutes late getting out at the end of the day. This was because he made us practise the final scene about twenty times, until he was happy we weren't the 'worst rabble of nincompoops I've ever seen in my life'.

By the way, the final scene was seriously bizarre, even by the standards of the rest of the play. In it, the Raisin King and two of the raisins have a candy-cane fight against the Emperor of Mars and the Evil Queen on top of the mince pie, which is hurtling towards the Sun. While they fight, the rest of the class have to chant: 'We're all going to die. We're all going to die.' Again and again.

I have no idea why any of this happens, but I wouldn't describe it as being very Christmassy.

In the middle of the fight, the lights are meant to go out and the play suddenly stops. Mr Le Gonk said this is so that the audience will go home not knowing whether Christmas has been saved or not. 'Keep 'em confused,' he said.

Well, they'll definitely be confused, I thought. Nobody could possibly have a clue what was going on. After watching two hours of that dribbling nonsense, most of the audience would have forgotten their own names.

Oh yes, and you read that correctly by the way. Mr Le Gonk's play was TWO HOURS long. 'When you captivate an audience,' he said, 'they will stay with you, hypnotised, for as long as you want them.'

Hmmm. I wasn't sure about that. Our original song and dance lasted about three MINUTES. On Friday, all of the other classes in the school would have to perform as well. The production would end up going on all night at this rate.

Finally, Mr Le Gonk clapped his hands together three times. 'Right. That's enough.'

'And I'm out of here,' said Miss Clegg, legging it out of the door, her coat already on.

'Go home. Learn lines. Remember the fundraising Christmas market is tomorrow, so put up your posters around the local area,' said Mr Le Gonk, waving a huge pile of photocopied posters and a box of drawing pins. 'Oh. And there will be a before-school rehearsal, at seven o'clock in the morning.'

Everybody sounded deeply thrilled about this.

'What?'

'No way?'

'Oh man!'

Seven o'clock? In the morning?! I didn't even know there *was* a seven o'clock in the morning. This was child cruelty. What would he do next? Peel off our eyelids? Stick chopsticks up our noses? Make us wear Gamble's underpants over our faces?

'Do we have to come even if we don't have a speaking part?' I asked as I collected my pile of posters and drawing pins off him. The afternoon had been a complete waste of time for me. I'd spent the whole time either standing on the stage doing nothing or sitting on the floor watching the rest of the class being weird. I didn't see the point of doing it again when I could be in bed.

Mr Le Gonk glared at me. 'Of course. You need

more practise than anyone. You were the least convincing person pretending to be a chewed-up pea I've ever seen.'

I wondered how many other times he'd seen someone pretending to be a chewed-up pea.

'Parents will be emailed,' he snapped. 'Now begone.'

On the way out of school, I remembered I had a couple of quid in my bag, and I needed something to cheer me up.

Squidgy Splodge had brought out a special Christmas range of doughnut flavours. Most of these actually sounded horrible: Mince Pie Magic was one (a doughnut that is actually a mince pie in disguise – imagine how disappointing *that* would be). Then there was the Tinsel-tastic Turkey and Gravy Flavour, and Santa's Sprout Surprise. *Yuck* and *double yuck*.

However, they had also created the Chocolate Log Supreme (a raspberry jam doughnut wrapped in a thick layer of chocolate), which was pretty much the greatest thing in the history of the universe – greater than air. Greater than the Sun. Greater than internet videos of squirrels falling out of trees.

Maybe I should buy myself a little reward for sticking up these posters, I thought.

'Fancy coming to the shop?' I asked Vanya. 'Doughnuts are on me.'

Before she could answer, Gamble swooped in ahead of her. 'Nah. I've got stuff to do, innit.'

I don't really like it when Gamble says he's got 'stuff' to do. Normally this means he's going to do something dangerous or disgusting or illegal. Or all three. Like that time when he spent an entire weekend training his pet dog Scratchy to fart on policemen.

'What kind of stuff?' I asked suspiciously, even though I hadn't been talking to him in the first place.

'Stuff for the fundraiser tomorrow,' he said. 'I've got things to buy online. You'll love 'em.'

The following day, of course, I'd find out exactly what he was going to buy. And I definitely would *not* love them.

Feeding the Pigeons

On the way to Gibson's, Vanya and I spent most of the time talking about Mr Le Gonk. 'He's horrid,' she said, pinning our twentieth and final poster to a telegraph pole.

'Except to Mr Noblet and Rosie,' I replied.

'Hmmm. It's obvious he's just *pretending* to be nice to them. He doesn't seem to be very good at acting.'

'I wonder what this *big production* was that he's just been in,' I said.

Vanya sniffed. 'I dunno. I searched on the internet last night and there was nothing about him anywhere. He can't be *that* famous an actor.'

I frowned. This *was* strange. If he'd been in all the plays and films that he *said* he had, then surely his name would've been *somewhere* online.

'I'm going to ask him tomorrow,' she said. 'Now let's go grab those doughnuts!'

When we arrived at Gibson's, I was absolutely gutted. They'd just that minute completely sold out of Chocolate Log Supreme doughnuts. And then I spotted Rosie. She had a giant bag of Chocolate Log Supremes and was feeding them to some pigeons. This was just about the worst thing anyone could possibly do. It was like buying a beautiful picture, then painting over it in black so that nobody else could look at it.

I felt like crying. 'What are you doing?'

Rosie smiled smugly, breaking the last piece of

doughnut in two. 'I overheard you saying you were coming here to buy a doughnut. Thought it'd be fun.'

'Why would you do that?' asked Vanya, as a particularly fat pigeon swallowed about half a doughnut in one go.

Rosie threw the last morsel on the ground for the pigeons to fight over. I was genuinely tempted to join in with them, but Rosie stopped me by wiping her sticky hands down the front of my jumper. 'I realised I hadn't been cruel to you all afternoon, Roman, and I was starting to miss it. I feel a lot better now.'

'That's my girl!' called her dad through the window of his Range Rover. He's a rich businessman, and he thinks that being nasty to people is a good way of showing them who's boss. One time he had a woman thrown out of his shopping centre because she had an 'offensive smell'.

Shoulders slumped, we trudged inside Gibson's. All they had left in the Squidgy Splodge cabinet were a couple of Mince Pie Magics and a slightly crushed Santa's Sprout Surprise. We turned around and shuffled out again.

I was disappointed to leave empty-handed, but

there was no way I was going to eat the sprout one: what kind of person would CHOOSE to eat vegetables? I'm not a nutter. And as for mince pies, well, they'd already caused enough damage.

Although that was nothing to what they'd do to me on Wednesday.

WEDNESDAY

Morning

The Play Changes and Mr Noblet Finds Out Who's In Charge

The next morning, I showed up at school bleary-eyed for the early rehearsal, clutching a tin under my arm.

The tin was all Mum's fault.

I'd told her about the early morning rehearsal when I'd got back from Gibson's on Tuesday night. I was hoping she might've told me that I didn't have to go.

I was seriously wrong.

She'd been so excited that she'd practically done a back flip.

'Ooooooh, my baby boy,' she cooed. 'A real-life,

proper actor, doing early morning rehearsals and everything. You're my super-duper little superstar.'

She's pretty much the most embarrassing person on the planet.

'I don't want to go,' I said.

'But why not? This could be your big chance of fame!'

I shook my head. 'I don't think so. I'm playing a half-eaten pea.'

Mum clasped her hands together. 'Imagine that! My son! A half-eaten pea! I've never been so proud!'

'I don't even have a single word to say.'

'Everybody's got to start small,' she said, waggling my cheek. 'What about that famous actor, George Moony? Didn't he start off by playing a singing satsuma in a children's TV show?'

'How should I know? Anyway, why do I have to go to the rehearsal? I could be doing something more useful. Like sleeping. Or eating doughnuts. Or putting my socks in alphabetical order.'

'The *rehearsal* is useful. You've got to impress your new teacher.'

'He HATES me though.'

'I don't believe that. Who could hate my icky wicky Roman emperor? I tell you what – I'll bake some mince pies for everyone in your class to give them energy for the rehearsal.'

'But I don't like mince pies.

'Nonsense! You love them.'

And that was that. There's no point arguing with her when she's in that kind of mood.

Early Rehearsal

So that explains why I had a tin of warm mince pies with me when I trudged into school at seven on Wednesday morning.

SEVEN! It was still DARK outside and FREEZING COLD, and the caretaker had to open the front door to let us inside.

We were all milling around in the classroom, not knowing what to do, when Mr Le Gonk scampered in. His chubby body was squeezed into a purple velvet jacket. He had a black beret perched on top of his ridiculous hair, and he'd drawn a beauty spot on the side of his face. I didn't bother asking why.

'You are all here,' he said, puffing out his chest, 'because yesterday's rehearsal was the worst thing that has ever happened to me.'

'The *worst* thing ever?' asked Vanya, who's never

frightened to stick up for herself. '*Really?* The worst thing that's *ever* happened to you is a bunch of kids practising your play?'

Mr Le Gonk stared at her. 'Yesterday . . .' he said. His voice was soft and cold, like a wolf creeping through snow, 'I had to watch as you *destroyed* my beautiful work.'

'It wasn't all that good to start with,' muttered Vanya. She's not normally *quite* this rude, but she doesn't like mornings, and she *really* didn't want to be there at all.

Mr Le Gonk didn't seem to hear her. He was fully performing now, as if he was onstage. He took a deep breath, his bottom lip wobbling. 'That play was my baby. I had given birth to it.'

'Oh gross!' I said. It was *way* too early in the morning to think about disgusting stuff like THAT.

'*Can* men even give birth?' asked Vanya.

Still he went on, glancing towards the sky. 'You took my baby. And you . . . flushed it down the toilet. You may as well have ripped out my heart!'

With that, he fell to his knees, and began pounding the floor with his fists and screaming: 'WHY? WHY? WHY?'

This was seriously uncomfortable. We all glanced at each other.

'Wow! That is so strange,' whispered Vanya.

I had to agree with her but there was something quite horrible about all this. Mr Le Gonk was now curled up into a ball, making these little sobbing noises like a hungry mouse.

I crept over to him. 'Are you . . . OK?' I asked.

To my surprise, Mr Le Gonk suddenly leaped to his feet. 'Of course I am all right, you fool. I was ACTING. That was an acting lesson. And you just learned from a highly experienced actor how to control an audience. You all felt sorry for me, didn't you? Didn't you?'

Vanya sniffed. 'Not . . . *really.*'

Gamble put his hand under his armpit and made a trumping noise. '*I* felt sorry for you.'

'Thank you, child,' said Mr Le Gonk.

I gave Gamble a surprised look. Gamble doesn't normally feel sorry for anyone. He shrugged back at me. 'Mrs McDonald told me to be nice to him so I'm gonna be, innit.'

'I felt sorry for you too,' I said to Mr Le Gonk. I don't know why I said this – I guess I was just hoping he'd stop hating me. It didn't work.

Mr Le Gonk tutted. 'Well, who cares what you think, *Sprinkler*?'

'Sprinkler?' I asked.

'Yes. Sprinkler. It's your new nickname.'

I'd never had a nickname before. I'd always wanted a cool one, like 'Turbo Legs' or 'Shadow Ninja' or 'The Doughnut Dude'. But *Sprinkler*? Trust me to get an awful one like that. It made me sound like the kind of kid who always wees on his own shoes.

'You're the one who made sure the school wasted all its money on fire safety instead of spending it on my play,' said Mr Le Gonk. 'So henceforth I shall only call you Sprinkler.'

'Yeah, Sprinkler,' said Rosie.

Oh great, it was catching on.

'I brought mince pies,' I offered pathetically.

'You should've brought some talent, Sprinkler,' mumbled Mr Le Gonk.

Ouch.

Rosie Taylor applauded loudly. 'Well, Mr Le Gonk, I think you were marvellous. Bravo! Bravo!'

Mr Le Gonk bowed to her. 'Right, well, Sprinkler has wasted too much of our time already. And – thanks to him **again** – we'll be wasting even more time later holding our Christmas market when we could be rehearsing. Let us begin at once.'

Parcels

Mr Le Gonk wouldn't let anyone have one of the mince pies I'd brought until after the rehearsal. He said the pastry would dry out people's mouths. 'I remember doing a play with Dame Maggie Flunk,' he said. 'She ate a jam tart beforehand, and her throat got so dry it fell out onstage.'

'Her *actual* throat fell out?' whispered Vanya, shaking her head at me. 'I bet he's never even *been* in a play. He's making it all up.'

'What was that?' asked Mr Le Gonk, staring at her. I gulped but Vanya remained cool.

'Ahem,' she said, 'Mr Le Gonk, I was just wondering about your acting career. What *was* this big production that you were recently starring in?'

Mr Le Gonk's reaction was quite surprising. For a moment, his face went white. His lips narrowed. He looked seriously uncomfortable. Then he kind of twitched, and a big sausage smile spread across his face. 'Oh, you won't have seen it, darling. It was French.'

'Ah,' said Vanya, '*parlez-vous français?*'

Although Vanya's dad is Indian, her Mum is French, so she speaks it really well.

Mr Le Gonk looked at her in compete confusion.

'I asked if you speak French,' Vanya said flatly.

'I knew that,' muttered Mr Le Gonk angrily. 'And yes, I do. I just don't have time to do it now, that's all.'

He stomped off.

'See,' said Vanya, once he'd gone, 'he's lying. I'll bet he's never acted in his life.'

We went to the hall straight away. We were allowed in there before school because the sprinklers weren't being fitted until nine o'clock (you know, the kind of time that normal people start their day).

The rehearsal was even worse than yesterday's. Mr Le Gonk seemed tetchy after what Vanya had said. Plus he kept changing his mind about how things should be done. He'd say things like: 'How about the raisins all speak with Welsh accents?' or, 'Try that again, but this time pretend you've got a hunchback,' or, 'Can somebody please just chew Sprinkler's leg or something? He *really* doesn't look half-eaten enough.'

The whole thing was getting more confusing by the minute. It'd been bad enough yesterday, but none of us could keep up with the changes. Nobody had a clue where they were supposed to be or what they were supposed to be saying. And Mr Le Gonk was getting angrier and angrier the whole time.

'No, you buffoon!' he yelled at Kevin *Puke Skywalker* Harrison. 'You're the Raisin King. You're meant to *wear* that crown, not hold it on your knees.'

Kevin gulped. 'Sorry. But I had to rush my breakfast. And I feel like I might . . . you know . . .'

Mr Le Gonk clasped his hand over his forehead. 'That crown once belonged to William Shakespeare. If you are sick into it, I will call the police.'

Kevin winced.

William Shakespeare? As if.

'Now, back to the practice. You! Emperor of Mars,' said Mr Le Gonk, pointing at Vanya. He was being especially mean to her since she'd caught him out. 'Maybe we'll change this scene so that you say all your words backwards.'

Vanya took a deep breath. 'This is nuts.'

Just then the rehearsal was interrupted by Miss Clegg slobbing into the hall. She had two packages balanced in one hand and was eating a slice of pizza from the other. *A slice of pizza!* I looked at the clock. It was five to nine. Who on earth eats pizza at five to nine?

'What time do you call this?' asked Mr Le Gonk haughtily. 'The rehearsal began at seven o'clock. You were meant to be helping.'

Miss Clegg stuffed about half the pizza into her vast gob and then spoke as she chewed. 'Yeah. I know. But I decided to sleep in. Then I found half a pizza under my pillow and I thought I'd put it in the microwave and have it for breakfast.'

Microwaved pillow pizza for breakfast?

Yum yum.

Mr Le Gonk didn't seem to know what to say to this. Miss Clegg swallowed her entire mouthful of pizza then burped. 'Oh, and, Darren, some geezer on a motorbike just delivered these to reception. Said they're for you.'

'Yessssss!' hissed Gamble. He sprinted over to Miss Clegg and grabbed the packages out of her hand. Then, for no real reason, he kicked her in the shin.

There were two packages, both wrapped in grey plastic. One was large and soft-looking, about the size of a cushion. The other was similar in size and shape to a tomato-ketchup bottle.

'What are they?' I asked, as he came back across the room with them.

'They're for the Christmas market, innit. I bought 'em online last night. Next day delivery. You wait and see. You'll love 'em.'

At that moment, the woman from the sprinkler company came in, along with two workmen carrying tool bags. 'We're starting now,' she smiled. 'Gotta make this place safe from fires.'

'We might as well go back to the classroom now anyway,' sighed Mr Le Gonk. 'The play's not going to get any better.'

Mince Pies

When we'd trooped back to the classroom he clicked his fingers. 'Sprinkler. The mince pies. I feel hungry after watching that Clegg woman stuffing her face like a pig.'

I got the tin and handed out the mince pies. Mum had stayed up half the night baking them. She'd decorated each one individually, with the person's initials done in pastry. Most people were pretty impressed and grateful.

Note the use of the word 'most'.

'I'm not eating *that*,' said Rosie, curling up her nasty little mouth in disgust. 'They're way too fattening. I can't look like a blob onstage when the TV and film people come to watch me. Plus I wouldn't touch anything that your mother's filthy fingers have been near. *Hashtag*: GOW – Grim Old Woman.'

Rolling my eyes, I went to offer her mince pie to another person, but Rosie wouldn't let me. She said she wouldn't dream of poisoning anyone else with it, then threw it in the bin.

Mr Le Gonk barely looked at his before tossing it straight into his mouth. 'Not bad, Sprinkler,' he said, spraying crumbs out everywhere. 'Four out of ten.'

After I'd been round everyone, I flopped back in my seat next to Vanya, with my mince pie on the table looking up at me. Even though I've told her a million times that I hate them, Mum had made me a massive one the size of a dinner plate. On it, she'd written in pastry:

Mummy

♥

Roman

'That's sweet,' said Vanya, nodding at it.

'Embarrassing, more like,' I replied.

Suddenly Gamble was in front of me, his tiny little peanut head bobbing around all over the place. 'You gonna eat that? Can I take it? Please-please-please!'

'Sure,' I said. 'Why not?'

He snatched it off the table and shoved it under his dirty polo shirt. 'I'll bring it back later.'

'Eh?' I said. 'Aren't you going to eat it?'

Gamble grinned at me. 'Nope. You'll see, Roman. You'll see.'

I shook my head. What kind of a person *borrows* a mince pie and brings it back later? *Then again*, I thought, *this* is *Gamble we're talking about*. One time he came round my house and borrowed a pair of my underpants without asking. He brought them back – *used and unwashed* – three days later. I don't want to go into too much detail about what state they were in after he'd worn them, but I will say that Mum wouldn't allow them in the house – she made Dad burn them on a fire in the garden.

EAT IT!

After we'd finished the mince pies, Mr Le Gonk told us we needed to turn our classroom into a 'rehearsal space'. We all hauled the tables and chairs outside and left them in the corridor. The first scene we worked on was the one when we meet the Evil Queen.

'Nyah ha ha!' cackled Rosie, rubbing her hands together. 'I am so evil!'

She didn't need to be in character to say this.

'Yesterday,' she continued, 'just for fun I threw pepper in a kitten's eyes. And today, I will ruin Christmas. Nyah ha ha!'

She ruins every day, I thought to myself.

I turned to Mr Le Gonk, and was surprised by his reaction. He was weeping – seriously, *weeping* – and mouthing the words along with her, as if this was the most beautiful thing he'd ever seen. 'Perfect,' he said, clutching his hands to his heart, 'utterly perfect.'

Eh? It was so unfair that he was praising Rosie

when he was being so horrible to everyone else. She thinks she's amazing, but when she acts she really goes over the top – pulling all these faces and straining her voice as if she's on the loo.

Just then, Mr Noblet came into the classroom. 'Ah, Mr Le Gonk,' he said, 'I hope you don't mind me interrupting.'

'Why would I?' said Mr Le Gonk, huffing out his cheeks. Yesterday, he'd been really working hard to be polite to Mr Noblet, but today he seemed to be finding it difficult to hide his irritation. 'What is it now?'

'Three things, actually,' said Mr Noblet, wringing his hands together. 'Firstly, you haven't done the register . . .'

Mr Le Gonk raised one bushy eyebrow. 'I am busy with rehearsals. Plus I am a trained actor. I should not be wasting my time on boring administrative tasks.'

'Well. The register is important,' said Mr Noblet, 'I mean – what if there was a fire?'

'Fire – fire – fire,' said Mr Le Gonk, pretending to yawn. 'It's all you ever talk about. Change the record. May I remind you that we're only rehearsing in here because the hall is out of action due to your precious "fire safety". And the second reason why you ruin my rehearsal . . . ?'

Mr Noblet paused and held his breath. He seemed genuinely surprised that Mr Le Gonk was being rude to him.

'I thought it'd be nice if the children made a get-well-soon card for Mrs McDonald.'

'Absolutely not. She *deserves* a long spell in hospital after the terrible job she did with the play before I got here. Item number three . . .'

'Ah – erm – well – it's the tables and chairs that you took out of this room . . .'

'What about them?'

'You've put them in the corridor. They're in the way of a fire door. And on top of that, the children can't get past to – *you know* – go to the loo.'

'Good grief,' said Mr Le Gonk, leaping to his feet. 'They should train themselves not to need it. When I was performing *That's Not My Egg!* at the Grand Theatre in London, I was onstage for seven hours. And if I needed the toilet I just did it right there in my tights.'

Too much information.

'Now please leave my rehearsal, sir!' he barked, hands on his hips.

Red blotches were beginning to appear on Mr Noblet's cheeks. He was obviously struggling not to get angry. 'Mr Le Gonk. You are being rather rude to me. Other teachers have also complained an—'

'We are getting closer to the performance,' said Mr Le Gonk snootily. 'This is not the time to be polite and nice. Tempers will rise. Other people must learn to deal with it.'

'But . . .' said Mr Noblet.

'Mr Noblet,' simpered Rosie, sliding in between him and Mr Le Gonk, 'I know that you're the head teacher and whatever. But remember, my daddy is a school governor. And he's sort of your boss.'

'Well . . . not quite but . . .'

'And my daddy wants Mr Le Gonk to be my teacher because he knows that Mr Le Gonk will make me look good in the play and that will make me happy. So kindly leave him alone and let him do his job, OK?'

She said this last bit in a horrible, sing-song voice, with her horrible slug's bum smile stretched across her horrible head.

Mr Noblet opened his mouth a few times to start talking, his moustache dancing around like a poodle on a pogo stick, but he didn't seem able to find the words.

Mr Le Gonk turned away from him and clapped his hands together. 'Right, everyone, scene five. Let's go. But this time we'll try the whole thing in Norwegian.'

For a moment, Mr Noblet stood there, all limp and floppy like a wet vest on a washing line. I felt sorry for him. He obviously didn't know what to say. Eventually he kind of drifted out of the room and left us to it.

I wasn't in scene five, so at first I felt quite happy to have a rest from practising.

Note the words 'at first'.

The people onstage were on the eighth run-through of the scene. After the sixth go, Mr Le Gonk had decided he didn't want it in Norwegian any more (mainly because nobody knew Norwegian and they were all just saying 'hurdy gurdy hurdy gurdy' for all their lines). Now he was trying to get people to yodel their lines instead. Unfortunately, none of them could really yodel either and Mr Le Gonk was getting more and more agitated with them.

Just then Gamble traipsed into the room. I

realised I hadn't seen him for at least five minutes

'Where have you been?' yawned Miss Clegg as he passed her. She hadn't gone looking for him or anything – she'd been too busy on her phone, shopping online for new bras.

'None of your business, monkey-face,' snapped Gamble. Then he sidled over to me and shoved my mince pie under my nose. 'Here y'are. Have this.'

I recoiled from it. 'No, thanks. I don't like them.'

He shoved it at my mouth. 'EAT IT!'

Very slowly, I took it off him and bit into it. It's not a good idea to say no when Gamble tells you to do something. Like that time when I wouldn't give him my last Mini Cheddar so he filled my shoes with wet cement.

I took a small bite. The mince pie tasted a little strange. And not just in a mince pie way. There was something different about it. Something *medicine-y*. What on earth had he put in it? I went to spit it out into a tissue but, before I could, Gamble had grabbed my jaw, and pulled my mouth open. He stuffed a load more of the mince pie into my mouth. Then he clamped his filthy hand over my lips and put his fingers up my nostrils.

It was awful.

On top of the terrible smell of his fingers and the weird taste of the mince pie, I couldn't breathe.

'Mmmfffh mhhhh mppphhhh,' I said, beginning to panic.

'If you want to live, the only thing you can do is chew it up and swallow,' he growled into my ear, not letting go.

So I did.

And it was the worst mistake I have ever made.

At the start, I said that mince pies were the worst thing about Christmas. There's no doubt that this is true. If I hadn't swapped my Fruit Pastilles for Gamble's mince pie – and if we hadn't been to see those actors in the panto – none of this would've happened. Mrs McDonald wouldn't have been set on fire, Mr Le Gonk wouldn't have turned up with his insane ideas, and I wouldn't have ended up with a nickname that made me sound like I had a watering can for a willy.

But maybe 'the worst thing about Christmas' wasn't quite strong enough.

Because, from Wednesday afternoon onwards, I

would learn that mince pies were worse than this. They could be deadly, like explosions. Or tigers. Or exploding tigers.

Things were about to get seriously serious.

Afternoon

We Raise Money for the Play and I Grow Up VERY Quickly

I should have known that something bad was going to happen. For the rest of the morning, I couldn't shake Gamble off. He was all over me like a really bad case of fleas. Every two minutes, he kept shoving his face right up to mine and staring at me. He hadn't looked so intensely at something since Mrs McDonald brought in that caveman book with the pictures of naked ladies in it.

Every time he looked at me his face would crumple in disappointment, and he'd say something like 'Still nothing' or 'What a waste of twenty quid' or 'Come on, Roman, get on with it.'

Get on with what? What was going on?

It was strange and confusing, and I didn't like it one little bit.

I was pretty certain that it had to have something to do with the mince pie he'd given me. *But what?*

Unfortunately, I'd find out very soon.

We were having our lunch sitting on the classroom floor. The hall was out of bounds because of the sprinkler system being fitted, and our tables had now been moved to a storage shed outside.

The rest of the morning had carried on much like before – Mr Le Gonk trying to make his play even more crazy than it was already, then getting angrier and angrier when nobody knew what he was talking about.

Lunch was spaghetti Bolognese with chocolate mousse for dessert. I don't eat spaghetti Bolognese any more, ever since an unpleasant incident involving Gamble's dog's worms. I just had a bowl of mousse.

I was halfway through eating it when Vanya suddenly dropped her fork onto the floor. There was a look of shock and horror on her face. 'Oh, Roman,' she said, her hand over her mouth, 'I don't want to worry you but . . .'

Hearing her, Gamble scrambled over on all fours, his knee going right into my mousse.

'Yes!' he screamed, grabbing my face for the three-millionth time that day. 'YES! The first sprouts of Christmas! I knew it! We're going to make a fortune at the Christmas market.'

I frowned at him. Sprouts? Fortune? What on earth was he talking about?

'I'll get a first-aider!' said Vanya, jumping to her feet and running out of the room.

A first-aider? But I wasn't ill . . . *was I?*

'This is brilliant!' Gamble continued, prodding at my jaw. 'I can SEE it coming out! Here. And here. And another one here! I knew this was the right way to do it!'

By now, my face had started to feel strange. A prickly heat was building up rapidly in my cheeks. It became more and more painful until I felt like I'd fallen face first into a patch of nettles.

What was going on?

Then other people were surrounding me, eyes wide open as they peered up close to my face and said things like 'Wow!' or 'Cool!' or 'Urgh!' I felt like an exhibit in a museum.

I put my hand to my face. It was red hot and tender, and it felt like . . .

Hang on.

No.

That wasn't possible. It couldn't be.

I sucked my spoon clean and looked at my reflection in it. What I saw nearly caused my brain to fall out of my head.

I was growing a beard.

Santa

Seriously. A beard. It was so freaky. Great tufts of silky fur were sprouting out across my jaw and chin. I could *see* it growing before my eyes.

Unable to speak, I just stared at my distorted reflection in the back of the spoon, watching helplessly as the beard grew longer and thicker.

Within five minutes my face was completely covered in hair.

'Perfect!' said Gamble clapping his hands. 'You look just like Santa! You're gonna smash it at the grotto this afternoon!'

I tried to reply but the only sound I could make was, 'Mubble wubble.'

What had he done?

The beard didn't stop there. It was still growing. And so was the hair on my head, which was creeping and curling towards my collar and over my eyes. I looked like a Viking.

'How?' I finally managed to say.

Gamble held up a bottle and sloshed the contents around inside it. 'Put it in the mince pie, innit!'

I snatched the bottle off him and, holding the fast-growing hair out of my eyes, I desperately scanned the label:

BALD AWAY!
Extreme Anti-Baldness Cream

'Anti-baldness cream?' I whispered. 'Extreme?'

'Yep!' said Gamble proudly. 'Bald men put it on their heads, so their hair grows back.'

I continued to read.

Contains 10,000 treatments

Instructions:
1) Mix one drop with a litre of water.
2) Massage into bald scalp.
Hair will regrow overnight.

WARNING!
EXTREMELY POWERFUL – DO NOT EXCEED
RECOMMENDED DOSE. ALWAYS MIX WITH
WATER. DO NOT USE STRAIGHT FROM BOTTLE.
ONLY USE ON AREAS WHERE YOU WANT HAIR
TO REGROW.

DO NOT SWALLOW.

This product has not
been tested on humans.

Lots of things on the label made me very worried indeed.

First of all, it had never been tested on humans. *So how was I supposed to know if it was safe?*

And the bottle was almost half empty. *One drop was enough to make your hair grow back, but I must've had nearly 5,000 doses.*

And Gamble hadn't mixed it with water. *No wonder my hair was growing so quickly.*

But, worst of all . . .

'It says I shouldn't have swallowed it,' I said, anxiously tugging on my beard, which was now halfway down my chest.

Gamble waved his hand at me. 'Mnyeh. Thought it might work quicker if you swallowed it, and I was right! Look at you – you've got a lovely hairy face.'

I was starting to really panic now. 'But there must be a reason *why* I shouldn't drink it. What if it's poisonous?'

'Don't be soft. I bought some last month for my grandma. Scratchy licked a few drops up and *he* didn't die.'

'Scratchy's a dog,' I said, ignoring the mental image of Gamble's hairy grandma. 'And he only had a few drops . . .'

'Yeah,' Gamble laughed. 'He got a proper hairy tongue though.'

Unbelievable. 'Why would you give me this stuff?'

Gamble grinned at me. 'For the grotto of course. I need you to look like Santa – otherwise nobody'll believe you're him. Bought it off the internet. It's totally illegal in this country.'

He seemed quite pleased about this.

'Oh great. It's illegal. Is that meant to make me feel better?'

'Huh! Loads of things are illegal that are actually really good – nuclear bombs, shoplifting, badger-wrestling.'

I slapped my hand across my eyes. The kid is absolutely nuts. 'This isn't *really good*. I look like a werewolf.'

'Oh,' said Gamble, looking hurt. 'I thought you'd like it. I got it delivered to school this morning with your Santa suit.'

I took a few moments to let this sink in. 'Hang on. You bought me a Santa suit? What's wrong with a *fake* beard?'

Gamble frowned. 'Oh *yeah*! I didn't think of that.'

Fantastic.

But it didn't stop there. Within ten minutes, the hair had spread to my forehead, my neck and under my clothes. My hands and wrists were becoming hairy. Little curly wisps were poking out from my chest above the collar of my polo shirt.

Rosie sauntered past. She didn't look surprised at all. 'Oh – you're turning into a gorilla at last, Roman. I always knew that you hadn't fully evolved into a human. At least we can't see your gross-tabulous face any more. *Hashtag*: big improvement.'

Just then, Vanya came back with Miss Clegg. Miss Clegg is the school first-aider, but she's absolutely rubbish. First of all, she's got big clumsy banana fingers, so she always makes your injuries worse. Plus, well, she's not a very nice person.

'What's all this about?' she moaned, puffing from the effort of walking into the classroom. 'I was *trying* to eat my sausage butty and . . .'

She stopped in her tracks when she saw me.

Now I'm not an expert on how to be a good first-aider. But I'm pretty sure there are some things that a first-aider is NOT meant to do when looking at someone who needs help:

1) Don't scream.
2) After you've finished screaming, don't say, 'OMG, that is disgusting!'
3) **Definitely** don't start taking photos and uploading them onto Facebook while saying: 'My friends are gonna freak out when they see this!'

'Aren't you going to help him?' said Vanya.

Miss Clegg rolled her eyes. 'Fine. Whatever,' she groaned, putting her phone away. 'Right. Let's call your mum. I ain't dealing with it – you'll put me off my sausage butty.'

As Miss Clegg led me through the classroom, everyone stared at me. We got to the door just as Mr Le Gonk was scuttling in.

'What is going on here?' he snapped.

'Roman's decided to turn into a yeti,' said Miss Clegg.

'What an awful thing to do!' said Mr Le Gonk, turning to me. 'You've ruined the play.'

'*Me?* I didn't *want* to look like this,' I said.

Mr Le Gonk didn't seem interested. 'Hmmm . . .' he said, tapping his teeth. 'I suppose I could rewrite the script. Instead of a half-chewed pea, maybe you could be a boiled sweet covered in fluff that Santa had found down the back of the sofa and eaten when he was hungry. Might work . . .'

'Why does it matter what I am?' I said. 'I don't even speak in the play.'

'Be quiet. You've already caused enough trouble.'

'But I told you, it wasn't me.'

'I did it!' said Gamble cheerfully. 'Look!'

He held up the bottle of BALD AWAY to Mr Le Gonk, who took it off him and read the label. 'Right. Well. I'll have to confiscate this. I can't have all my actors wandering about like chimpanzees.'

'Awww,' said Gamble, 'I was gonna use that. I've always wanted hairy eyeballs, innit.'

Mr Le Gonk ignored him and turned to Miss Clegg. 'So where are you going with this furry boy?'

'Call his mum. Get her to bring a collar and lead and walk him home.'

She laughed like a broken washing machine at this, but I didn't find it funny. Neither did Mr Le Gonk. 'Well, make sure he's back here for the fundraiser. We need everyone here to help raise money for this play, even if they do look like a total freak.'

'I'm still here, you know,' I said grumpily.

Mr Le Gonk didn't hear me. He'd trotted off to his desk and was putting the bottle of BALD AWAY into his briefcase.

A thoughtful look came over Gamble's face. This is never a good sign. He doesn't usually think at all unless he's plotting something terrible: like that time he decided to hide a wasps' nest in Miss Clegg's handbag.

'What are you planning?' I asked, parting my droopy moustache so I could speak.

Gamble stared off into the distance, barely seeming to hear me. 'Total freak, eh?' He scampered off after Mr Le Gonk and began whispering to him.

So Proud

I followed Miss Clegg to the office, where she rang my house. On the way there, people were staring and pointing and laughing at me. It was absolutely humiliating. Within ten minutes, Mum had burst into the school. When she arrived, she took one look at me and her knees seemed to buckle beneath her.

'Oh, what's happened to my gorgeous baby boy?' she cried, leaning against the wall for support. 'Your beautiful face. Ruined forever!'

I huffed out my hairy cheeks. To be honest, I wasn't that good-looking to start with.

She pawed at my beard. 'Right. We're going home right away and I'm going to strip you off and shave you immediately.'

'Shave me?' I said. 'I'm not a sheep.'

She began leading me out of the door. At that

moment, Mr Le Gonk burst into the reception and barrelled over to us. 'Ah, my dear lady!' he crooned, putting on his super-friendly act again. 'How marvellous to meet the mother of such a fine young actor.'

'Eh?' I said.

Mum loosened her grip on my shoulder. 'Fine actor, you say?'

'Oh yes! I've promoted him to the key role of a hairy boiled sweet in the play.'

An impressed smile spread across Mum's face, and she seemed to forget about the beard for a moment. 'Ooh. Really? You didn't tell me, Roman.'

What was going on here?

Mr Le Gonk straightened his belt. 'Oh yes. Now I hope you're not thinking of getting rid of this luxuriant beard . . .'

'Well . . . I . . .' said Mum.

'Because,' continued Mr Le Gonk, 'I was just speaking to your son's young friend, Darren. He told me how Roman here *bravely* grew this beard to help us raise extra money for the school play.'

'Really?' said Mum.

'Really?' I said.

'Oh yes. Darren says that Roman has had a wonderful idea for this afternoon.'

'Did you?' asked Mum.

'Did I?' I asked.

'So surely we should wait till the end of the week to shave it off,' said Mr Le Gonk. His voice was a soft, persuasive purr. 'It will give him the chance to *save* the play *and* have a starring role in it.'

Mr Le Gonk squeezed my shoulder.

I didn't like this one little bit.

'I don't think so,' I said. The beard was seriously itchy and made me look like something a cat had coughed up.

'We need you,' said Mr Le Gonk, putting a chubby knuckle between his teeth and pretending to look anguished.

'Well . . .' said Mum, who was somehow being taken in by this rubbish. 'I mean . . . If you put it like that.'

'And might I say, he does suit a beard,' said Mr Le Gonk. 'He looks like Sir Terence McGrunt, the finest actor of all time.'

Mum giggled. 'Oooh yes. You're right. And I suppose it *is* pretty amazing that he can grow a beard in the first place. He *is* only ten.'

'You must be so proud,' smarmed Mr Le Gonk.

'Oh, I'm always proud of my Romy Womy,' she said. 'Whatever he does.'

'How sweet,' said Mr Le Gonk, who had very slowly removed Mum's hand from my shoulder and was now leading me away. 'We'll see you this afternoon for the big fundraiser.'

'Wouldn't miss it for the world,' called Mum, as he bustled me out of the foyer and back towards the classroom.

This was getting weird. What had Gamble told him?

Of course, I would learn this soon enough.

I'm Not Doing It

'I don't care,' I said. 'I'm not doing it.'

It was one hour later. The fundraiser was about to start. Gamble and I were standing in the filthy, disgusting caravan that Gamble's uncle Terry had towed onto the school field for us to use as Santa's Grotto.

But Gamble had changed our plans for the fundraiser. We weren't doing Santa's Grotto any more.

Gamble tutted. 'Oh, come on, don't be rubbish. Why won't you do it?'

'Because,' I said, 'number one – I don't want to wear this nappy . . .'

I held the nappy up in the air. *Where on earth had he got a nappy that was big enough for me to wear?* Actually, scrap that, I didn't want to know.

'You'll look great!' said Gamble.

I wouldn't, by the way. My whole body was completely covered in long, curly hair. And when I say covered, I *mean* covered. Honestly – my bottom looked like Albus Dumbledore. The only good thing was that at least it'd stopped growing now.

I ignored him. 'And number two – I don't want to be part of a freak show.'

'It's not a freak show . . .' said Gamble, twitching angrily. 'It's a *Caravan of Mutants*.'

'Well, that makes it OK, doesn't it?'

He didn't notice my sarcasm. 'Just do it or I'll have to pull off your ankles.'

'Fine,' I sighed. I knew he wasn't joking. 'But there's no way I'm wearing the nappy.'

'You've got to wear the nappy – you're the

Bearded Baby. We can't have a caravan of mutants without a Bearded Baby.'

'I didn't want to have a Caravan of Mutants in the first place,' I said, exasperated.

'But nothing says Christmas like a bunch of deformed monsters,' he said, looking hurt. 'I nicked out of school especially to advertise it.'

He was wearing a huge sandwich board over his shoulders that read: 'TWODAY AT SCOOL. MEAT THE BEARDED BABBY. HE'S A PROPER WEERDOW!' Apparently, he'd sneaked out of school for the rest of lunchtime, parading around the local area with it.

'I'll be here too,' said Vanya supportively. She was wearing a vest and had a moustache painted onto her upper lip. She'd agreed to join us in the caravan and be the 'World's Strongest Girl' so that I wouldn't feel too bad.

It was a nice gesture but it wasn't really working.

At that moment, Mr Le Gonk burst into the caravan. 'Are you ready? The fundraiser is about to open. Remember – big smiles. We need all the money we can get.'

I rearranged my nappy. 'I'm not really sure about this . . .'

Mr Le Gonk waved me away. 'Nonsense. The Bearded Baby is the star attraction. You were born to play this role.'

Born to be a hairy freak in a caravan. That just about sums me up.

And right then, our first customers arrived.

The Caravan of Mutants

Being in the Caravan of Mutants was seriously awful. First of all, my fur was really itchy and hot, and at one point I got some caught in the Velcro of my nappy.

Far worse than the pain though was the total, crippling embarrassment. Gamble forced me to sit on the floor, sucking on a dummy. He then made me say, 'Goo goo ga ga, baby need a pee-pee,' every time someone came in.

It was awful.

The adults and the older kids from our school were bad enough. They'd point and laugh say things like, 'Good grief!' or 'Look – it's Chewbacca's little brother!' or 'Could you lend some hair to my husband? He's as bald as a bowling ball.'

But the younger kids were a million times worse.

They were so thoughtless and mean. They'd yank on my fur or burst into tears. One of them even said, 'Mummy, why is that doggy so fat?'

Thanks a bunch.

Still, my least favourite moment was when my mum came in. I've already told you that she is the most embarrassing person in the universe. 'Oh, I'm so proud of you!' she trilled, stroking my shoulder like I was some kind of giant hamster. 'Still in primary school and you've already got a lovely beard. My little boy is a man.'

Give me strength.

The only good things were:

1) Vanya. When things were becoming too stressful, she'd step in front of me and lift up some 'extremely heavy' weights (really just empty boxes on either end of a broomstick, painted to look like barbells). This would at least take the attention away from me for a few moments.

2) Thanks to Kevin *Puke Skywalker* Harrison, we had to close our stall early. He came in to see us while he was on a break from his banana-milkshake-on-a-trampoline-challenge stall. He took one look at my furry body and took several deep breaths. 'I don't like it!' he moaned, clutching his

belly and gulping. 'I've drunk nine glasses of banana milkshake and they're jumping about in my belly.'

I don't really want to talk about what happened next. Luckily Gamble, Vanya and I were able to take cover under a table while Kevin redecorated the rest of the lounge in a horrific shade of yellow.

'Nice one, Barf Vader,' said Gamble as we crawled out afterwards.

Barf Vader! Even though it'd been completely disgusting, and the caravan now smelled like a cow's unwashed udders, I quite liked this new nickname for Kevin. It was good to keep the Star Wars theme going.

'It was always gonna happen,' Kevin said sadly, 'You just look so . . . *gross*, Roman.'

When the pukiest kid in Europe thinks you're gross, then you *know* you've got problems.

At least by the time this happened, it'd all been worth it and we'd raised some serious money for the play.

Er, well, by 'serious money' I actually mean thirteen pence.

It would have been more, but we had to give one of the dads some money after Kevin ruined his shoes. Oh, and Gamble kept a fiver for himself because, in his words: 'I'm saving up cos I wanna have my hand chopped off and get a metal claw fitted in its place.'

Over the course of the afternoon, we had precisely nine customers. Well, eight, actually. One of those was the same person. She returned to get her watch, which Gamble had stolen off her wrist the first time around.

All in all then, it'd been a complete waste of time. Feeling pretty dismal, I put on my uniform and headed out of the stinky caravan.

Well Done

After the fundraiser had finished, we went back to the classroom. It was nearly four thirty. Mr Le Gonk wanted to talk to us before we went home with our parents, who were waiting outside.

'So,' boomed Mr Le Gonk, 'I have counted up all the money you made this afternoon. And you managed to raise –' he paused, tilting his head back and looking down his nose at us – 'three thousand, one hundred and four pounds and twenty-seven pence. So well done!'

Everyone seemed quite pleased with this, and they began chattering excitedly to one another.

'Yes,' continued Mr Le Gonk, his deep voice silencing the room. 'Well done, you incredible people. You've *really* done yourselves proud.' He clapped his hands loudly and slowly. 'What a *tremendous* effort. I couldn't be *more* impressed.'

'Hmm. Do you think he's being sarcastic?' I whispered to Vanya.

'Just a bit,' she replied.

Mr Le Gonk took a deep breath through his nose. 'You have all let yourselves down once again. Apart from Rosie, that is.'

Rosie gave one of her horrible tight smiles. She looked like a worm sucking a lemon. 'I raised three thousand pounds selling signed photos of myself,' she smarmed. 'Yes. It turns out that the public adore me.'

'She only sold one,' whispered Vanya to me. 'Her dad bought it.'

Three thousand quid to have a picture of Rosie! Wow! I'd pay three thousand pounds NOT to look at her horrible face.

'This is not enough money,' continued Mr Le Gonk. 'Thanks to Sprinkler over there, we needed to raise at least three hundred and fifty thousand pounds to make this play a success.'

It wasn't fair that he kept blaming me. I mean, OK, so it was me who'd suggested the sprinkler system to Mr Noblet. But come on! As if Mr Noblet would've given him that much money for the play in the first place.

'I thought you said that you needed two to three hundred thousand pounds for the play,' said Vanya, sticking up for me.

Mr Le Gonk scowled. 'That was before I decided to put in the spaceship, the laser show and the giant robotic insects.'

'Giant robotic insects?' mouthed Vanya to me. 'What a nutter!'

I tried not to giggle but I couldn't help it.

'SILENCE!' yelled Mr Le Gonk. 'This is not a moment for comedy. We need another three hundred and forty-six thousand, eight hundred and ninety-five pounds and seventy-three pence. And we need it immediately. Otherwise my dreams will be shattered. Does anybody have any further ideas?'

Everyone looked at each other. Where were we supposed to get that kind of money from?

'We could shave Roman's hair off and sell it to

make wigs for camels,' suggested Rosie. 'Then we could sell his body to a dog-food company. They could slice him up, stew him and put him in tins. *Hashtag*: succulent chunks of meaty butt-head.'

Mr Le Gonk seemed to give this idea serious consideration. 'Hmm. The question is, would he raise enough money?'

I ground my teeth together.

'How about, instead of this big expensive performance, we just do a normal play? Or a short song and dance?' asked Vanya. 'You know, without all this crazy stuff that doesn't make any sense.'

A couple of people nodded and made 'sounds good' noises.

At this, Mr Le Gonk stood frozen to the spot, clutching his heart, his face twisted in horror. When he finally spoke, his voice was rough and forced, like he had a cheese grater in his throat. 'You mean . . . go back to the . . . *garbage* that you were practising before.'

'Yes. Exactly that!' said Vanya, her hands clasped together.

'I cannot believe my ears,' muttered Mr Le Gonk to himself, while pacing back and forth. 'Explain yourself!'

'I don't want to be rude,' said Vanya, 'But . . . well . . . the performance is meant to be fun. And entertaining. And only a few minutes long. I'm sorry, but I just don't think your play is any of those things.'

Mr Le Gonk spluttered. 'How . . . dare you?'

Rosie sprang to her feet. 'Shut your crusty gob, Vanya! Mr Le Gonk is the best thing that's ever happened to this school and we are doing his play. Got it!?'

'Thank you, dear child,' said Mr Le Gonk, holding his hand out towards Rosie. Then he gathered himself together. Hoisting up his belt, he stood legs apart and announced, 'Tomorrow is the dress rehearsal. We will make this work. Seven o'clock again. Do not be late.'

Vanya huffed out her cheeks. 'Well. I tried . . .'

We all shuffled out of the room to our parents. When I got outside, Mum bounded over and grabbed me in a tight hug. Then she turned to Mr Le Gonk. 'I'm just wondering if there's anything I should do to Roman's hair.'

'Madam,' said Mr Le Gonk, raising one bushy eyebrow, 'I am a distinguished actor, not a dog groomer.'

'But I don't want other children to tease him about it.'

Mr Le Gonk half-laughed. 'Oh, that won't happen.'

'Oh, wonderf—'

'No, no. There are lots of other things that the children could tease him about.'

It took me a moment to realise that he wasn't being very nice here.

Just then, Gamble came over. 'All right, Mrs Roman's mum,' he grinned. 'Don't worry. I've ordered some proper good hair removal cream off the internet, innit. We'll have Roman completely bald in no time.'

'I'd rather not be *completely* bald,' I said.

Gamble ignored me. 'It's called Fluff Away. It says it'll turn a polar bear into a polar bare. Geddit? Bare! I ordered it online with my dad's credit card.'

'Very kind of you,' said Mum.

'It'll be delivered next Monday.'

'Next Monday?!' I cried. 'I can't go round looking like this all week. Someone will put me in a flipping zoo.'

Gamble sniffed. 'Well, I've got my penknife. I could at least trim your face.'

'Definitely not,' said Mr Le Gonk, 'I can't change the script again. I need my fluff-covered boiled sweet to be hairy until after the final performance at least.'

Rosie Taylor strutted towards us and gave Mum one of her sickliest smiles. 'You really can't shave Roman before the performance, Mrs Garstang. We need everything to be perfect. Did you know that Mr Le Gonk is inviting some of his friends to watch the performance? They work in TV and films, you know.'

'Really?' said Mum.

Mr Le Gonk lazily waved a hand at her. 'Well – one has many friends in the entertainment industry. One meets so many people when one is an actor.'

'It's part of the reason why my dad gave him the job,' said Rosie. 'Mr Le Gonk promised that his friends who work in film and TV would come and watch me perform in the play. They'll probably be so impressed that they'll fly me to Hollywood to star in films, or give me my own TV series or something.'

Unlikely . . . I thought.

'Oooh! Who knows?' said Mum. 'Maybe they'll be impressed by you too, Roman!'

Mr Le Gonk laughed like a broken toilet. Then he realised she wasn't joking and he stopped.

'Not unless they're making a film about things that look like dog's bum-fluff.' Rosie muttered, her face twisted in a cruel smirk.

'What was that?' asked Mum.

'I said *Roman makes a wonderful hairy boiled sweet*,' smarmed Rosie. '*Hashtag*: fur-bulous, darling.'

Mum wriggled with excitement. 'Oh, thank you, Rosie. Well, I promise to keep him furry until Friday then!'

Great, I thought.

'TV and film people, eh?' said Gamble, cocking his shiny little head to one side. 'Is that right?'

THURSDAY

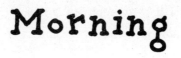

Morning

Mr Le Gonk Loses It
and Gamble Gets Busy

Wednesday night was horrible. Mum rang Grandma to proudly tell her how grown up I was looking all of a sudden. Grandma asked Mum if she could have the hair 'after I'd finished with it'. Grandma likes to knit. Apparently, she'd run out of wool for a cardigan she was making. I wasn't keen on this idea at all.

Plus it turns out that being hairy is generally very unpleasant. Firstly, I was roasting hot – it was like being wrapped in a thick, scratchy sleeping bag. As a result, Mum suggested that I take off my T-shirt. But then at tea time I got loads of food caught in my fur, which was disgusting. Trust me, nothing kills your appetite like finding a sticky lump of macaroni cheese in your hairy belly button. I could barely even manage my fourth doughnut after that.

Things got worse at bedtime. I couldn't sleep. Not only was I over-heating, but when I did finally fall asleep, I had a dream that I was turning into a were-donkey. I woke up sweating in my bed at 3 a.m.

Unable to get back to sleep, I decided to do a silly thing – I took out my tablet and googled 'Bald Away Anti-Baldness Cream'.

I immediately wished I hadn't.

Here's a good lesson: if you're worried about something, DO NOT EVER search for it on the internet. The internet is basically just a massive pile of information designed to scare the bejesus out of you.

I found out some terrible things. There was an article about how Bald Away had been banned in forty-eight countries. This was after some people showed 'alarming side effects' after using it. These side effects included: 'loss of teeth', 'rotting of the head' (I tried not to think about this one too much), 'blueness of the skin' and (perhaps most worryingly) 'some mild feather growth'.

By the way, I'm not sure how *any* feather growth on a human could be described as 'mild'. Surely even one feather would be pretty serious, wouldn't it? I can't imagine a doctor saying, 'Don't worry, Mrs Garstang. Your son might be turning into an ostrich but it's only a mild case. Just tip a spoonful of Calpol down his beak and he'll be fine in the morning.'

At the end of the article, it said that 'these side effects *were* rare and only affected 0.001% of users of Bald Away'. This should've made me feel better, but it didn't. 0.001% was a small chance but it *was* still a chance. It was bad enough being hairy, without worrying that Gamble had fed me five thousand doses of something that could turn me into a toothless, blue bird with a rotting head.

I stayed awake in bed, tossing and turning until the morning.

At seven o'clock on Thursday, I wandered yawning into school with Vanya. The rest of the class was slowly gathering in the hall.

'Are you OK?' she asked. 'You look terrible.'

'Thanks,' I replied. 'I haven't grown any feathers, have I?'

Vanya looked at me. 'No. Just the, er . . . *fur.*'

'Phew!' The article had said that all of the terrible side effects happened in the first twelve hours after taking it. I felt like I was safe. Hairy but safe.

The End

The sprinkler system had been fitted now so we were allowed back in the hall. There were little red shower heads dotted all around the ceiling. These shower heads were connected to pipes, which led to an enormous water tank that'd been put into the caretaker's office.

In the case of a fire in the hall, a heat sensor would turn on the sprinklers and put out the flames. They were going to be fitted around the rest of the school the following week.

When most of the class had arrived, Mr Le Gonk strode in and stood above us on the stage. Today, he was wearing a purple cloak and one of those hats that monkeys wear when they're playing the cymbals.

His face was grave. 'I have reached a difficult and . . . *terrible* decision.'

'You're going to stay on and teach us for the rest of the year,' whispered Vanya under her breath.

I sniggered.

'This afternoon was supposed to be our dress rehearsal,' he continued, not hearing her. 'But, due to a lack of money, caused by Sprinkler over there . . .'

Everyone turned to face me. Beneath my beard, I felt myself turning red.

'I have decided that . . .' He looked up, jutted out his chin and swallowed back a tear. 'Our play must be cancelled.'

Most people went *yesssssss!*

Except for Rosie, that is. She went absolutely banana-crazy. 'What do you mean *cancelled*? What about my big break? What about the film and TV people? You wait till I tell my father. He'll –'

'Alas,' said Mr Le Gonk, 'how can we do my script justice without proper funds?'

'Can we do the "Brussels Sprout Boogie" instead?' asked Vanya.

Mr Le Gonk looked as though she'd just asked him if we could dance around the stage naked with chicken nuggets balanced on our heads. 'Good grief, no. How could I inflict such utter trash onto an audience? No. You will not be performing anything.'

'*Awwwww!*' whined the class. '*Not fair!*'

Rosie was already on the phone to her dad, demanding that he call the police immediately and have Mr Le Gonk arrested for 'murdering her dreams'.

The rest of the class were muttering to each other and throwing their arms up in the air and looking generally fed up.

Clearly, most people hated his crazy play, but they wanted to do *something*. Not me though. I was the only person who felt happy about this decision. I was delighted that we weren't going onstage.

This feeling didn't last for long.

My happiness was interrupted by a *BEEP-BEEP-BEEP* noise from outside. A dirty blue transit van was slowly reversing towards the fire doors at the back of the room.

Mr Le Gonk strode to the back of the hall and flung the door open. 'What is the meaning of this?'

Just then, the doors at the back of the van opened up. Darren Gamble was standing in the back of it, surrounded by what appeared to be an enormous mountain of rags.

'Not missed anything, have I?' he grinned.

Gamble Saves the Play

Gamble's uncle Terry hopped out of the driver's seat of the van. Between him and Gamble, they hauled the mountain of rags out of the van and into the hall, dumping them in the middle of the floor in front of a speechless Mr Le Gonk.

When they'd finished, Uncle Terry clapped his hand onto Mr Le Gonk's shoulder. 'Whatever happens, you didn't get these from me, got it?'

Mr Le Gonk looked completely bewildered.

Before jumping in his van and speeding away, Uncle Terry ruffled Gamble's hair and told him to 'be good'.

Yeah, right – Gamble's idea of being good is to only chop off one of your arms.

Mr Le Gonk went over to the pile of rags and began picking items up. There were all sorts of things there – pirate outfits, sparkly princess dresses, even a banana costume. 'Where did you find all of this?'

'I can't tell you that. It's a secret, innit,' said Gamble, tapping his nose. But then he kind of ruined this by adding: 'But if you must know, Uncle Terry broke into the theatre in town and robbed the costume department.'

It's probably worth saying here that Gamble's uncle Terry is a serious criminal. As well as many other things, he's been arrested for robbing shops, beating up cars (not the drivers, notice, but the *cars*), and kidnapping. In fairness to Uncle Terry, he didn't realise he was actually kidnapping someone. They just happened to be using a portaloo at the exact moment when he stole it from a building site.

I gulped – this wasn't good. Among all of the other clothes, I recognised Madame Boom Boom's towering blue wig from the pantomime we went to.

Vanya put her hand up. 'Mr Le Gonk. I don't like this. I think we should call the pol–'

'Absolutely not!' said Mr Le Gonk.

'But my mum is the chief of police for the whole city,' said Vanya. 'If she finds out we're using stolen clothes she'll go mental.'

'But what is the worse crime?' asked Mr Le Gonk,

squinting at her. 'Stealing a few outfits, or letting down your audience?'

'I think we've already been through this,' sighed Vanya.

Mr Le Gonk raised a finger in the air. 'We will return them after the play.'

'After the play?' I asked, horrified. 'But I thought that the play was cancelled.'

'Nonsense!' said Mr Le Gonk.

Rosie hung up her phone call. 'Are you saying . . . ?'

'It appeared that my masterpiece would be lost forever,' boomed Mr Le Gonk, puffing out his chest. 'But this strange little fellow has shown us that, with the right spirit, the show can and must go on!'

Most people sighed or groaned as his words echoed around the room. The only person who looked pleased was Rosie. 'Yes, Mr Le Gonk! Yes! That's the spirit!' she cried. 'The TV and film people will love me in your play! *Hashtag*: watch out Hollywood.'

Mr Le Gonk leaped back up onto the stage. 'Who needs a giant model of a burning comet, when we can *ACT* one out? Who needs a wall made of ten million raisins when we can *ACT* one out? Who needs explosions and costumes and lasers when we can *ACT* them out? Tomorrow, you are going to act like your lives depend on it! And you are going to shine!'

I gulped and looked around nervously. Almost everyone else seemed worried too. One more day till the performance, and most of us still didn't have a clue what we were doing.

Only Rosie looked totally happy. 'I can't wait to share your wonderful play with the world!' she simpered.

Mr Le Gonk raised his monkey-hat to her. 'Many people said that this play would fail. They said that the world was not ready for such a powerful piece of theatre.'

'They were right,' yawned Vanya.

I giggled nervously.

'Choose your costumes, actors,' he said. 'We have but five hours to prepare for your dress rehearsal in front of the whole school!'

At least this was popular. Everyone dived into the mountain of clothes and began grabbing things at random. Nobody seemed to care exactly what they were wearing: dresses, army uniforms, top hats, gorilla suits, robot outfits.

'Yes! Yes!' cried Mr Le Gonk. 'Choose anything you can get your hands on. Let's really make the audience *think*.'

Yes, I thought, poking around for something that would cover the whole of my hairy body. *The audience will **definitely** think. They'll think:* 'Why is Santa dressed as a cowboy? And how come the King of the Raisins has a horse's head?'

Rosie was holding up a sparkly ball gown in front of herself. 'I'd hug you . . .' she said to Gamble, 'if it wasn't for the risk of infection.'

Gamble farted proudly.

There was something very strange about this. Why had Gamble suddenly gone to all this trouble? Why did he care if the play was a success or not? What was going on?

Of course, I didn't have to wait for long before Gamble explained.

'How can I repay you?' Mr Le Gonk asked him, patting him on the shoulder.

Gamble's head twitched excitedly. 'Let me be in charge of special effects in the play.'

Mr Le Gonk narrowed his eyes at him. 'O-kay. And why would I do that?'

'Well,' said Gamble jiggling about, 'you said you've got people who work in film and TV coming to watch tomorrow.'

Mr Le Gonk raised a bushy eyebrow. 'Yes . . .'

'When I grow up I want to blow things up and set things on fire and that.'

This is true by the way. Or at least partly true. Gamble has several dream jobs for when he's older. They include: 'blowing stuff up', 'being a zombie' and 'kicking people'.

'So,' Gamble continued, 'if I do really well with the special effects, and I do loads of mad explosions, maybe the TV and film people will give me a job, innit.'

Mr Le Gonk frowned. 'But where will you get everything you need for all of these special effects? Thanks to Sprinkler we have no money.'

A creepy smile spread across Gamble's face. 'Amazing what you can get on the internet. If you know where to look. And if you've nicked the right credit card. I was proper busy last night . . .'

Gamble Is Left Alone

The rest of the morning was spent practising in the hall. Mr Le Gonk wanted the play to be perfect before we showed it to the school.

Occasionally another class would turn up. The teacher would ask if they could have five minutes to run through their song and dance one last time before the dress rehearsal.

'Of course you may not,' replied Mr Le Gonk each time. He seemed to have given up on even pretending to be nice to other members of staff. The teachers would stand there for a few moments, not really sure how to respond. Maybe they didn't want to argue with another adult in front of their children. Maybe it was just the way that Mr Le Gonk spoke. His voice was so powerful and final that they couldn't help doing what he said.

Whatever it was, they'd all do the same thing: turn red in the face then slope off with their class trooping behind them.

Meanwhile, Gamble stayed in the classroom with Miss Clegg. A series of different packages were delivered to the school office for him during the morning. I had no idea what was in any of them. However, as one package was being carried past the hall, I noticed a great big skull and crossbones on the side of it. It either contained something dangerous or some pirates.

At about quarter past ten, Mr Le Gonk sent me back to the classroom to get him a pencil. He wanted to change the script for the four trillionth time. From now on, Santa would occasionally shout the word 'APRICOTS!' for no apparent reason.

I'd given up on wondering why any of this was happening.

When I got to the classroom, I found Miss Clegg drinking a coffee and flicking through a clothes catalogue called 'Big-Boned and Beautiful'. 'Where's Darren?' I asked her.

Miss Clegg didn't look up from the catalogue. 'Cupboard,' she said, bored.

I looked over to the cupboard. The door to it was closed. 'What's he doing in there?'

'Don't know, don't care. I'm just letting him get on with it. First bit of peace I've had in ages.'

'Oh,' I said.

It isn't a good idea to leave Gamble alone to just 'get on with it'. He always ends up doing something naughty. Like when he got the job of setting up the music before people come into assembly. Alone in the hall for twenty seconds, he changed the CD from 'Peaceful Soul Moods', to a heavy metal song called 'Excruciating Leg Amputation' by Dr Pain and the Bloody Stumps. Two of the girls in Year One had to have counselling afterwards.

Anyway, back in the classroom, it didn't take long for something to happen.

There was a sudden loud bang from inside the cupboard. Then, curls of green smoke began creeping out around the door frame.

'Sick!' said Gamble from behind the door.

Completely unmoved, Miss Clegg took a gulp of coffee and turned the page of her catalogue.

I backed away and out of the room.

Screaming

I was halfway back to the hall when I first heard the shouting. It was loud and uncontrollable, like a mad pelican trying to escape from a sack. What on earth was going on?

I nervously opened the hall door and my eyes nearly popped out. Mr Le Gonk was yelping and screeching wildly. He was leaping up and down on his hat, which was now as flat as a pancake. His enormous hair was sticking up all over the place, his face was bright purple, and spit was flying out of his mouth in all directions.

'WHY!' *jump* 'CAN'T!' *jump* 'YOU!' *jump* 'JUST!' *jump* 'DO!' *jump* 'IT!' *jump* 'RIGHT?!'

In front of him, Kevin *Barf Vader* Harrison looked ready to cry. 'B-b-but I don't know what you mean . . .'

'I TOLD YOU!' yelled Mr Le Gonk. There was a vein on the side of his forehead that looked ready to burst. 'YOU'RE THE *RAISIN KING*. TRY TO SOUND MORE LIKE DRIED-FRUIT ROYALTY! HOW HARD CAN IT BE?'

Kevin clutched his stomach. 'I think I need to be sick.'

Mr Le Gonk yanked at his hair with both hands and let out a piercing scream. I've never seen a teacher lose it like that. Everyone else in the class was staring at him with their mouths open. I thought he might actually pick Kevin up and boot him off the stage like a football.

Luckily, at that moment the playtime bell rang. 'RIGHT! Get out, the lot of you! OUT!!!!'

As we hurried outside, I asked Vanya what was going on.

'I don't know,' she said, 'He just flipped out over nothing. He's getting way too stressed about this play.'

'Er. No, he's not,' said Rosie, butting in as usual. '*I* don't think there's anything wrong with cracking a few skulls. The dress rehearsal is this afternoon. We can't afford to have useless skidmarks like Kevin ruining our performance, especially when I've got TV and film people coming in to watch me tomorrow. *Hashtag*: sort your lives out, fools.'

With that, she swanned off outside.

'I'm going to speak to Mr Noblet,' said Vanya, shaking her head.

The Rat

Apart from Rosie, nobody was in much of a rush to get back to the rehearsal after playtime. As a result, I ended up near the front of the line. When I got into the hall, I found Mr Noblet and Mr Le Gonk talking to each other by the side of the stage. At first they didn't see us.

'This is the *theatre*, darling,' sighed Mr Le Gonk. He'd calmed down a lot now, though his face was still red. 'We must do what it takes to make this play perfect. And if that means raising my voice once in a while, then . . .'

Mr Noblet ran his fingers across his moustache. 'But when I agreed to have you teaching this class, I didn't expect stolen costumes and crying children and upset teachers and . . .'

When Mr Noblet saw me and the rest of the class, his voice tailed away. He cleared his throat. 'Perhaps we should continue this chat later, Mr Le Gonk. Just please be more . . . calm. Now if you'll excuse me, I've got some fire blankets to order.'

He scurried off out of the room.

Once he'd gone, Mr Le Gonk pursed his puffy lips. 'Well, well, well,' he said. His voice was rich and dangerous, like a poisoned chocolate-fudge cake. 'I'd love to know which one of my actors scuttled off to whisper these terrible accusations about me.'

He tapped his tiny foot on the floor and glared at each one of us in turn. There was a horrible sickly thickness to the air, as if it'd been turned into soft cheese.

Vanya folded her arms and stepped forward. 'It was m—'

'Definitely Roman,' interrupted Rosie, 'He hates me and he wants the play to fail so that the TV and film people don't give me my own movie to star in. *Hashtag*: hairy little weasel.'

'Me?' I said. Yes, of course I don't like Rosie – she once spread a rumour round the school that I'm 'half-human, half-verruca'. But still, I didn't *want* the play to fail. And I wasn't trying to stop Rosie from becoming an actress – her own complete lack of talent was probably going to do that. I don't want to be mean, but I've seen soggy bits of Weetabix that are better at acting than she is.

'Actually, it was me who told Mr Noblet about you,' said Vanya defiantly. 'I don't like the way you treat people.'

She's easily the bravest eleven-year-old I've ever met.

Mr Le Gonk didn't seem to hear her though. He'd narrowed his piggy eyes, and he seemed to have drifted off somewhere else. 'Of course. Sprinkler. The nasty beast. I'm not surprised. He's already wasted our budget on fire safety and made me change the script with his furry body.'

He wagged his finger at me. 'I will not forget this.'

Vanya was getting red in the face now. 'I'm telling you it was m—'

'SILENCE!' bellowed Mr Le Gonk. 'Every play has its problems and its arguments. I remember being in *The Toothbrush Mysteries* with Sir Roger Balloon. He got so angry with one of the actresses during rehearsals that he pulled her still-beating heart right out of her chest.'

'Urgh,' I said. Despite this story being utter rubbish, it was still disgusting.

'The man is insane,' murmured Vanya to me.

Mr Le Gonk continued, staring straight at me. 'The most important thing is that – even if we hate someone, even if we want to get our revenge on them for the terrible things they've done . . .'

I gulped.

'. . . we NEVER let the audience know. The show must always go on.'

At that moment, Gamble came in. He was wheeling a trolley in front of him, which was covered in a sheet. 'Ta-dah!' he grinned, pulling the sheet off to reveal a random jumble of all kinds of weird stuff. Then he began picking things up off the trolley to show us. 'I've been proper busy making props and special effects, innit. Look: blood-soaked fake leg . . . smoke machine . . . red glowing eyeballs . . . cat sick . . . exploding gun-shot wounds . . . evil toilet . . . deadly mince pie bomb . . .'

I wasn't sure if any of these things would actually be useful for the play, but they certainly made Mr Le Gonk look happier. This was probably the worst thing about him – the way his moods could flip so quickly. It meant you could never trust him at all.

He patted Gamble on the back. 'Well done, dear boy. Good to see someone who doesn't want this play to be a total disaster.'

I noticed his eyes flicking towards me again when he said this.

'Ahem – what about me?!' said Rosie. 'I'm the star.'

Mr Le Gonk bowed to her. 'Of course, my dear. Of course.'

Rosie smiled her slug's bum smile.

'D'you think the TV and film people will be impressed when they come to watch tomorrow?' asked Gamble. 'I want 'em to give me a job, innit.'

'Huh,' yawned Miss Clegg. 'Can't imagine you

on TV. Unless they've just invented smell-o-vision and they're making a show about the inside of a whale's anus.'

Gamble stamped on her toe. 'Shut your noise, Bumbeard the Pirate. I'm gonna be proper famous, me.'

'That's the spirit,' said Mr Le Gonk, ignoring the first part. 'Now. We must rehearse like our lives depend on it. And . . .' he paused for dramatic effect, 'who knows? Maybe they do.'

Afternoon

We Blow the Audience's Minds and Gamble Tests the Sprinklers

Well, one thing is for certain: if our lives *had* depended on how well we practised, then we would all have been very, very dead.

In fact, the morning practice had been a complete mess. Mr Le Gonk had changed the play **again**, so that we could use all of Gamble's new special effects. Quite a lot of these changes involved me.

I was now an *evil* hairy boiled sweet with red glowing eyes, carrying a deadly mince pie. Before the raisins went through the portal on the flying mince pie (and no matter how many times I write this, I still don't quite understand what it means), the Raisin King had to shoot me repeatedly with a gun, then chop off my leg. None of it made sense, nor did it seem to move the story along. In fact, it was totally bonkers.

However, Mr Le Gonk seemed quite keen on me being badly injured. 'Yes! That's it! Really slice him with that saw!' he gleefully yelled at Kevin *Barf Vader* Harrison. 'And if he *actually* bleeds then the audience will believe it more.'

Kevin didn't look happy about it. 'I feel a bit rough.'

'Excellent!' cried Mr Le Gonk. 'Use it, boy! Use it! If you need to puke on him, just do it! It'll make the whole thing more real!'

'I'd rather you didn't,' I said.

Are You Ready?

Strangely enough, for once Mr Le Gonk didn't seem to think that the practice had been a mess. That afternoon, before we went through to the dress rehearsal, he seemed full of energy and excitement.

We were all wearing our costumes for the play. I was back in my nappy from the freak show. I didn't think that this made me look more like a

hairy boiled sweet. I just think Mr Le Gonk wanted
to make me miserable.

Other people were wearing whatever they'd dug
out from the costumes Gamble's uncle had stolen.
It didn't seem to matter what their characters were.
The Raisin King was dressed as a giant fish. The
lump of reindeer meat looked like a ballerina. Mr
Le Gonk thought that this was great – he seemed
to think that the play would be better if the audience
was totally confused about what was going on.

Only Vanya wasn't wearing a costume. Out of
principle she'd refused to wear the stolen gear, so
she was in her school uniform.

'We have worked hard,' Mr Le Gonk boomed.
'We have had problems. People have tried to ruin
our play . . .' Once again, his eyes rested on me at
this point. 'But now we have the chance to show
the world something that will blow their minds.
Are we ready, cast?'

Most of the class cheered. Mr Le Gonk's voice
had a way of building up people's excitement.

'Special effects technician, are you ready?'

Gamble burped.

'Then let us show this school what a real play
looks like!'

He swept to the door, with everyone lining up noisily behind him.

Dress Rehearsal

The point of a dress rehearsal is for everybody to practise in front of an audience for the first time. We had the parents coming to watch the next day, so our audience was all the pupils and staff from the school.

The hall was a weird sight, because all of the children were sitting in rows, wearing their costumes for the production. The Foundation Stage kids were at the front in their shiny wise men capes and home-made crowns. The Year Ones were struggling to sit down in their huge Christmas pudding costumes. Then there were other rows of angels, Christmas trees, Santas and so on.

Each class took it in turns to perform their little song, dance or sketch. My class were going last of all. As each of the other groups got up, I felt more and more nervous. It was like someone was blowing up a balloon inside my belly, which was getting bigger and bigger all the time.

There were two reasons for this. Firstly, like I

said before, I hate being onstage. I don't like people staring at me at all.

But, more importantly, the more I watched, the more I realised that all of the other classes were miles *better* than us. For a start, their parts of the show lasted for a couple of minutes each instead of about ten years, like ours did. The little kids looked seriously cute. The older ones had interesting, clever routines. There were funny jokes, lovely songs, well-planned dances. Everyone was smiling and happy and knew what they were doing.

Mr Le Gonk wasn't impressed with the other classes though. Occasionally he would yawn dramatically, or tut, or say something under his breath like, 'How embarrassing,' or, 'Who planned this monstrosity?'

And then it was our turn.

As the wild applause for the Year Five group (who did a really funny rap and dance-off dressed as reindeer) died down, Mr Noblet the head teacher stood at the front. 'Well, guys,' he said to the school, 'we've got one last super-great class le—'

He was interrupted by Mr Le Gonk bursting onto the stage, bowing and waving, even though nobody was clapping him. 'Thank you so much!' he boomed. 'So kind!'

The rest of the school stared at him blankly.

'We all enjoyed those . . . *basic* and *cute* performances,' he said, making 'basic' and 'cute' sound like two words you might use to describe a rash on your buttocks. 'But now for something . . . spectacular. I warn you. This play is so powerful that some of you might literally lose your minds.'

A few children tittered but Mr Le Gonk growled at them. 'I do not joke. Many audiences have become drooling vegetables after watching me act.'

For once, I believed him.

He clasped his hands over his heart. 'I only ask that none of you become jealous or sad about how your performances might look in comparison to this one. It is best not to compare. I am, of course, a professional actor . . .'

Mr Noblet coughed and pointed at his watch.

'Harrumph,' said Mr Le Gonk. 'Prepare to be astounded by *Inside the Mince Pie* by me, Bartholomew J. Le Gonk. Performed for the first time by my class, Year Six.'

The lights went down. From off-stage, a voice

came over the loud speaker. 'Imagine a world of pastry. Of mincemeat. Of DEATH.'

Then the play began.

Going to Plan

For the first ten minutes or so, everything went perfectly to plan.

Unfortunately, the plan was a confusing mess which nobody understood. As a result, the play was a complete disaster.

At the beginning, a giant sheet was meant to cover the whole audience and make them think they were inside a mince pie. Unfortunately, we hadn't been able to afford this. Instead, Gamble just threw handfuls of pastry and mincemeat into the crowd, which people had to dive out of the way to avoid.

The play had been changed so many times that nobody knew their lines or what was meant to be happening. The Raisin King started tap dancing for no reason. Two of the raisins had wandered off and gone to the loo when they were supposed to be onstage.

Meanwhile, Gamble kept setting off special

effects at random times. Every so often, a blood-soaked false arm would fly across the stage and smack someone in the side of the head, or there'd be a sudden sound of gunfire.

Only Rosie Taylor was doing as she was supposed to. That said, she *was* playing the Evil Queen, so she didn't exactly have to try very hard.

By now, the audience was getting restless. Most of them had stopped watching the play at all. They were talking or wriggling about restlessly.

Then it all went wrong.

A bored kid in Year Five picked up one of the balls of pastry that Gamble had chucked into the crowd and rubbed it into someone's hair. Then that person picked it up and threw it across the room. It arced lazily over people's heads and landed somewhere else in the audience. There was a lot of giggling, and someone threw it back. Then a handful of mincemeat globbed through the air and hit one of the Year Threes in the back.

Within seconds, the audience had given up on the play altogether. Missiles of pastry and mincemeat were being lobbed in every direction. Before we knew what was happening, the air was filled with flying food.

'Is this meant to happen?' Mr Noblet asked Mr Le Gonk urgently.

But Mr Le Gonk didn't answer. He watched, unable to speak, his face a frozen mask of horror, as the hall descended into a full-on food fight.

The weird thing was that the other teachers did nothing to stop it. They just sat there, arms folded, smirking at Mr Le Gonk. I guess they were still mad at him for how rude he'd been all week.

It was Gamble who put us out of our misery. But, of course, I got the blame.

It Worked

The mince-pie-snowball war was now totally out of control. Most of the kids in the school were involved, standing up to belt each other with pastry and mincemeat, and shrieking with excitement. The only ones who weren't taking part were scrambling over each other to get out of the way, or cowering on the floor.

Mr Noblet waded into the audience to stop them, his shirt covered in splats of gloopy mincemeat. 'Please . . . don't do that that . . . no . . .'

It was too late though. The place was out of control.

Onstage, Rosie Taylor was crying her eyes out. '*Hashtag:* STOP IT!' she yelled. 'This is my last chance to rehearse. I've got TV and film people coming tomorrow and . . .'

WHUMP!

A ball of pastry smacked her right in the chops, knocking her backwards.

At that moment Gamble appeared by my side. 'This is well good!' he exclaimed, his head bouncing up and down like a novelty pencil topper. He was wearing a backpack. It was connected to a long tube – like a vacuum cleaner – that he was holding out in front of him.

'What on earth is that?' I asked.

'Smoke machine!' he said. Then he took a run up to the edge of the stage, screaming: 'SPLASHDOWN!' before diving into the tangled mass of bodies in the audience.

I stood there, mesmerised. Most of my class had left the stage and joined in with the mince pie battle. Someone had found Gamble's bucket of mincemeat and was now chucking great handfuls of it out into the audience.

At the side of the room, Mr Le Gonk had staggered backwards and flopped into a chair.

'Well,' said Vanya, standing next to me, 'at least it's improved the play.'

I smiled, just as she pulled me out of the way of a flying lump of pastry.

Then, as we straightened ourselves up, her mouth dropped open. 'What the . . . ?'

I looked down into the audience and – *oh my word!*

Gamble was firing huge plumes of thick black smoke out of the end of his tube. 'Haha! Gotcha!' he screamed through the fog.

Nervously, I looked from Gamble to the red sprinkler shower heads in the ceiling. Something told me that this might be a really bad idea.

And it was right then that an alarm rang and it began to rain.

Instantly it was like being in the middle of a monsoon. Water sprayed down from the sprinkler system. Within moments my fur was absolutely drenched.

The mince-pie-snowball fight stopped at once. The teachers finally heaved themselves up out of their chairs and took the children out through the fire doors. Within minutes, we were all out on the field. I thought that my hair might freeze solid in the cold air.

'Nice one, Sprinkler,' said Rosie angrily. 'You ruined everything.'

'Eh?' I said, teeth chattering. 'How was that my fault?'

Gamble stomped over, seriously angry. 'Stupid fire safety,' he growled. 'I didn't even get to set off my deadly mince pie bomb.'

'Good grief,' I said.

A Big Decision

Mr Le Gonk didn't come outside during the fire alarm. Miss Clegg had to take our register. She didn't look happy about this – she hates doing anything that looks like work.

When we walked back inside, twenty minutes later, it was almost the end of the school day. We found Mr Le Gonk waiting for us in the classroom. Considering how terrible his play had just been, he seemed surprisingly upbeat.

'Come in, get warm,' he purred. I glanced at Vanya – you really didn't know what mood he was going to be in from one minute to the next.

'We have a saying in the theatre,' he continued. 'It'll be all right on the night. In other words, when we perform for the audience tomorrow, we will be PERFECT!'

'Well, not all of us,' smarmed Rosie Taylor, looking at me.

'And I know we will be perfect, because . . .' said Mr Le Gonk, licking his lips, 'I have decided that none of you will be in the play.'

There was a stunned silence.

'What do you mean, *none of us*?' asked Vanya.

Rosie Taylor ground her teeth together. 'But you told me I was a superstar! You told me you were inviting TV and film people to come to see me!'

I could see she was getting seriously angry. Her face was screwed up and creased, like a forgotten pair of underpants. I shuffled my chair away from her. You don't want to get too close to Rosie when she has a tantrum brewing. I remember when Mrs McDonald told her that she wasn't allowed to bring her pet pug to school in her handbag any more. Rosie screamed so loudly that one of the computer screens cracked.

'My darling, the film and TV people will still be coming . . .' said Mr Le Gonk. 'Just not to watch you, that's all.'

'But . . . but . . .' spluttered Rosie.

'Are you having a laugh?' growled Gamble. 'I'm meant to be doing the special effects. I'll chew your flipping face off!'

Miss Clegg had to grab the back of his collar to stop him from pouncing on Mr Le Gonk, who leaped up onto his chair like he was escaping from a man-eating snake.

'Hang on,' said Vanya. 'If *we're* not going to be in it, then *who* is?'

Mr Le Gonk dropped to the ground and took a deep breath. 'This has been a very, very difficult decision. But I have decided . . .'

He began to weep, but no tears came out.

'Stop pretending to cry and get on with it,' snarled Rosie. '*Hashtag*: no one cares.'

'I have decided,' said Mr Le Gonk, pulling himself together, 'that *I* will be performing the play on my own.'

'*What?!*' I cried.

I knew that Mr Le Gonk was an odd fellow, but this was absolutely nuts! This was *our* school

Christmas play. The whole point is that the children get to do it for their parents. He couldn't do it! It would be like Mr Squidgy Splodge eating all of my doughnuts.

'Are you sure that's a good idea?' asked Vanya.

'It's the only way I can be sure that it'll be good,' said Mr Le Gonk. 'I mean, you can still *watch*. And, young Rosie, of course you can still *meet* my friends who work in film and TV.'

Just then, the bell rang for the end of the day. Several people stood up at once and stormed towards the door.

'And where do you think you're all going?' asked Mr Le Gonk.

'To speak to Mr Noblet,' said Vanya.

'To speak to my dad,' snapped Rosie, pulling her phone out of her handbag.

'To find some explosive stuff to blow you up with,' said Gamble.

'To be sick,' said Kevin *Barf Vader* Harrison.

'And what about you?' said Mr Le Gonk to Miss Clegg, who was lumbering out of the room behind them.

Miss Clegg yawned. 'There's something I want to watch on Netflix.'

They were met at the door by Mr Noblet. Rosie, Vanya and Gamble started talking at him all at once. He raised his hands. 'Thank you, guys,' he said. 'Maybe you should go home. And Mr Le Gonk – perhaps we could have a word when everyone's gone . . .'

FRIDAY

Things Get Back to Normal

(For a While at Least) and
Our Play Makes a Big Splash

The next morning, Mr Noblet met us as we came into the classroom. 'Settle down, guys,' he said, his moustache drooping. 'Now, I'm afraid I have some bad news. After . . . everything that happened at the rehearsal – and after chatting to the other teachers and Rosie's dad – Mr Le Gonk will no longer be teaching you.'

Most of the class began cheering.

This wasn't a surprise. Mr Le Gonk was obviously

completely crackers, and most people were delighted to see the back of him.

Even Rosie seemed happy.

'Why are you smiling?' asked Vanya. 'I thought you loved him.'

'Oh please,' said Rosie, flicking back her hair. 'I was *using* him. It's what you do if you want to be famous: you trample on other people to get where you want to be.'

'Do you?' I asked. 'Sounds horrible.'

'And that's why some of us become stars and others end up in the gutter,' she said. 'Daddy found out that Mr Le Gonk was being sacked last night. So I made sure that we can still make the most of him, even if he isn't going to be here.'

'Oh really?' I asked.

Rosie pursed her little hamster's-nipple mouth. 'Daddy told Mr Le Gonk that if his friends from the TV and film industry weren't at the play this morning, he wouldn't be getting paid. They'll be here, watching me and loving me. And soon I'll be famous.'

'Good luck with that,' I said. In the dress rehearsal, I thought that Gamble's bucket of mincemeat and pastry performed better than she did.

Meanwhile, at the front of the class, Gamble

was rooting through the drawers in the teacher's desk. 'I knew it!' he snapped. 'He's nicked my hair growth cream, the horrible stinky bag of bum sweat.'

I couldn't think for a minute what Mr Le Gonk would want with a massive bottle of hair growth formula. Unfortunately, of course, I'd find that out soon enough.

But there were other things to worry about first.

'Who's going to be our teacher now?' asked Vanya. 'And what's happening about the play?'

Mr Noblet wrung his hands together. 'Well. I'm not sure about the play, but as for your teacher . . .'

At that moment, the classroom door opened and Mrs McDonald walked in, her coat over her shoulders and her broken arm still in a cast. 'Coo-ee, everyone. I'm meant to be resting but Mr Noblet called and I came straight he-*yooof*!'

She couldn't finish her sentence because Gamble had raced over and grabbed her tightly round the belly. I think he was being friendly, but it was more like the kind of hug a boa constrictor gives to a baby deer.

'Welcome back, miss. I love you so much!' he cried, wiping his snotty nose across her skirt.

'Oh ho! Thank you, Darren,' she said, trying to prise him off as gently as possible. 'And thank you for all of the cards and pictures you brought round to my house.'

'S'all right, miss,' grinned Gamble. 'Anything for you, miss.'

'Although I wasn't sure how you found out where I live . . .'

'Followed you home once, miss. Sometimes I like to stand in your garden in the evenings and watch you through the window.'

'Oh,' said Mrs McDonald, her mouth hanging open. 'And I wasn't sure *why* you had to deliver them at three in the morning every day . . .'

'I couldn't sleep cos I missed you so much, miss.'

'*Or* why you'd drawn me *quite* so many pictures of people having their arms, legs and heads chopped off.'

'I thought they might cheer you up, miss.'

Mrs McDonald swallowed. 'Oh. Well . . . er . . . thank you again, Darren.'

She was trying to sound grateful but she looked scared to death.

'Er, Mrs McDonald,' said Rosie, clicking her

fingers, 'don't want to stop the little love-fest between you and the creature from the black lagoon here, but we've got a play to do in two hours and time is ticking away. *Hashtag*: sort it quick.'

'Oh. Of course,' said Mrs McDonald, putting her hand over her mouth. 'What shall we do?'

Rosie smiled her nicest smile at Mrs McDonald. 'Well. There are lots of things you're good at, Mrs McDonald . . .'

Mrs McDonald blushed. 'Why that's very ki—'

'You know. Like combing your guinea pigs or whatever,' said Rosie. Then her face hardened. 'But let's face it – drama ain't one of 'em.'

'Oh.'

'So I think we should do Mr Le Gonk's play.'

Everyone groaned.

'Honestly,' Rosie continued, 'I don't mind if you lot don't want to do it. I think I could take on all the parts and just do it by myself.'

There was a lot of noisy chatter.

'How about we just go back to doing the "Brussels Sprout Boogie"?' I suggested over the noise.

Mrs McDonald noticed me for the first time and

staggered back, her eyes like saucers. 'Goodness, Roman. What happened to your face? You look like one of my guinea pigs.'

'You don't want to know, miss,' I replied.

'Hair removal cream's coming on Monday,' said Gamble.

'Right . . .' said Mrs McDonald, slowly taking her eyes off me. 'Well, I suppose, yes, we could go back to the "Brussels Sprout Boogie". If everyone agrees . . .'

A huge cheer went up around the room.

Only Rosie wasn't happy. She stood up and stamped her foot. 'O to the M and back to the G, you ridiculous bunch of trouser-slugs. You cannot be serious.'

'Oh, be quiet,' said Vanya.

'Right,' snapped Rosie. 'Well, I've got TV and film people coming to watch me at the play. If we *must* perform that crud-alicious song and dance, *I'm* being on the front row and everyone else has to sing quietly so that I can be heard.'

'And I need to do my special effects. I never got to use my mince pie bomb, miss,' said Gamble.

'Mince pie . . . *bomb*?' asked Mrs McDonald.

Gamble grinned. 'Yeah, miss. It's well good. I

want to show the TV and film people how good I am at making things blow up and that.'

Mrs McDonald cleared her throat. 'Isn't that a bit dangerous?'

'Not if you've got instructions, miss.'

'And *have* you got instructions?'

'Course I have.'

'Oh good.'

'I mean, they're in Chinese, so I can't understand them but, you know, at least I've got them.'

'Oh.'

So we had a couple of quick run-throughs of the song and dance in the classroom and, actually, it wasn't bad. I mean, it wasn't exactly *good* either but this was mainly Rosie's fault. Her dancing style was to elbow everybody else out of the way, and she sang loudly and completely out of tune. I'm not an expert but I thought she sounded like an aeroplane full of cats crashing into a toilet factory.

But still, despite Rosie, everybody seemed to know what they were doing and did it with smiles on their faces. Best of all, Gamble didn't set off his mince pie bomb in the classroom. He said he was saving it for the main performance. So, when we lined up to go to the hall at five to eleven, everybody was feeling confident and happy. Things were looking up.

For now at least.

Meditating

The hall was packed. The mincemeat and pastry had all been cleaned up, and the water from the sprinklers had been dried overnight by the caretaker. Carols were playing on the music system, and reflections from the flashing lights on the tree twinkled off the tinsel and decorations that hung round the walls.

The children had to squeeze in at the front, facing into the audience. The back half of the hall was taken up by rows and rows of parents on chairs. They were all holding up cameras, phones and iPads so none of them could really see. When I walked in, my mum and dad leaped up from their seats and started waving madly and blowing kisses at me. I forced a smile back at them.

Our class squashed into a tiny space in front of the stage. Everybody in the hall was fidgeting or chatting or turning around and waving. I'd made sure I was as far away from Gamble as possible.

He was clutching his mince pie bomb (which was about the size of a large plate) and he had a match behind his ear.

The bad thing about this was that I was one space away from the end of the row. Next to me on one side was Kevin *Barf Vader* Harrison (who always sits on the end *just in case*), with Rosie on the other.

I didn't know which one was worse.

I mean, Kevin always feels a bit ill when he's nervous (then again, he always feels a bit ill when he's not nervous as well). He kept burping right near my ear and saying things like, '*Uh-oh. That one was a wetty*,' which was pretty bad.

But Rosie was even more annoying. She was sitting with her eyes closed, *breathing* really loudly and saying these strange things under her breath, like, 'Hummanummanummanumma. Give me strength, universe. Give me strength.'

It was seriously off-putting.

'What are you doing?' I asked.

'I'm trying to block out all of the horrible, nasty things in the world,' she said. 'Like you, for example.'

I rolled my eyes. 'If I'm so bad, why are you sitting next to me?'

'Duh – so that I look even better than I already am,' she sniffed. 'Now, if you don't mind, could you just shut your disgusting gob and let me meditate, you unbearable scrut-ball.'

'Oh! You're *meditating*,' I said. I have to ignore it when Rosie insults me. At least ninety-eight per cent of the things she says to me are nasty. 'I thought you were having an asthma attack.'

She sniffed. 'That famous American actress Angelina Bumwad does it before she goes onstage.'

'Right. But why do you need to do it?'

'Wow! You really are unbelievably thick, aren't you? Look over there,' she said, grabbing me by the beard and yanking my head round painfully. 'See that man and woman on the front row?'

I struggled away from her. 'Yeah. What about them?'

'They're Mr Le Gonk's friends. You know – the people who work in TV and film. They're here to watch me smash it onstage.'

'Oh,' I said. Neither of the people looked particularly special to me. The man was wearing work trousers and a grubby polo shirt. The woman was wearing a tracksuit. 'They don't *look* like film and TV people to me.'

'Oh really. And how many film and TV people do you know?' she asked. 'They have to dress like normal people, otherwise they'd get mobbed by talentless nobodies who want a ticket to the big time.'

'Right,' I said. *Like you, you mean . . .*

I noticed they were sitting next to Rosie's dad. He was taking up two seats – one for him and one for his phone.

'They're my ticket to fame and fortune,' Rosie went on. 'So don't you dare ruin my big chance.'

I didn't want to be cruel, but Rosie's big chance was probably going to be ruined by the fact that she was completely rubbish at singing and dancing.

Just then, Mr Noblet hopped up onto the stage, and all of the chattering died down.

A Surprise Visitor

Twenty minutes later we'd watched the first four classes. All of the parents had *ooohed* and *awwwed* at the Foundation and Key Stage One kids. Then we'd had the Year Threes, who weren't nearly as cute but had still done a good job. There were two more classes to go, then it would be our turn.

By now, Rosie was getting seriously fretful on one

side of me, saying things to herself like: 'You've got this. You're the greatest. You *will* destroy the audience.'

On the other side, Kevin *Barf Vader* Harrison was huffing and puffing and completely green in the face. Mrs McDonald leaned down. 'Roman, would you like to go outside with Kevin for five minutes of fresh air before we go on?'

Answer: absolutely not!

The last time I did this, I had to buy new shoes.

Still, it had to be better than sitting next to Rosie. I stood up and followed Kevin as he staggered out of the room, bent double.

'I'll come too,' said Vanya from further along the row.

I was glad to have a friend with me.

By the time we'd got out of the room though, Kevin had already disappeared into the loos. Vanya and I just had to stand there, waiting for him to come out, while listening to the muffled singing from the hall.

It was then that I noticed something.

How weird, I thought. The door to the caretaker's room was half open. This door is never open any more, not since Gamble went in there the other month and drank a whole bottle of cleaning fluid.

The light was on inside the room, and someone was clinking around in there.

'Wasn't the caretaker in the hall?' I asked, nodding towards the door.

'Yeah, he was leaning against the wall at the back,' Vanya said, frowning.

In fact, all the staff were in the hall, even the lazy ones like Miss Clegg. So if it wasn't someone who worked here, then who was it?

'Let's have a look,' Vanya said.

I held her back. 'But what if it's an intruder?'

'Exactly,' she said, shaking me off and creeping forward.

I gulped. Sometimes having a brave friend isn't everything it's cracked up to be. Terrified, I followed her towards the caretaker's room.

Muffled applause drifted down the corridor. The Year Fours must've finished. That meant there was only one more class till we were on.

'We should get back,' I whispered.

But Vanya shook her head. 'Let's just have a peek. If there's a burglar in there, we can go and get help.'

From inside the caretaker's room, I could hear a whole load of different sounds. Something being unscrewed. The hollow glugging of liquid into a tank.

What was going on?

Then there was a splash of liquid hitting the floor and a whispered swear word.

It was a voice that I recognised.

Vanya slowly pushed the door open and we saw who it was.

'Holy doughnuts!' I whispered.

'You two?!' exclaimed a shocked Mr Le Gonk. 'What are you doing here?'

The Deadly Plan

From inside the hall, I could hear more applause. The Year Fives must've been getting up onto the stage.

'More like what are *you* doing here?' said Vanya coolly.

'Ah. Well . . .' stammered Mr Le Gonk.

I looked from the little pool of liquid on the floor to the bottle that Mr Le Gonk was holding. The label was half hidden by his chubby paw but I could still read what it said:

BALD AWAY
Extreme Anti-Baldness Cream

A horrible feeling built up in my belly. What was he planning on using that for?

And then I realised.

Mr Le Gonk was standing right next to a huge red water tank that nearly filled the whole room. The lid of the tank had been unscrewed and was sitting on the shelf next to it.

'You've poured hair growth cream into the sprinkler system?' I said in disbelief.

'If it goes off, everyone will end up hairy, like Roman,' said Vanya.

Sweat was beading on Mr Le Gonk's upper lip. He let out a nervous laugh. '*Hee hee*. Just a little prank. Teach these ungrateful pests a lesson.'

'A prank?' I asked, an unpleasant feeling building in my guts.

Mr Le Gonk was shaking. I couldn't tell if this was because he was scared or angry or a bit of both. 'They need to learn their lesson. You can't put fire safety ahead of a great play.'

'But that's . . . really cruel. And really *strange*,' said Vanya.

There was a mad twinkle in Mr Le Gonk's eye now. He was twitching, and his great tidal wave of hair had flopped over to one side. 'Oh yes. They'll pay. They'll pay for ruining my play. They'll pay for not listening to my ideas. And that Mr Noblet will pay for taking away my chance to finally go onstage and act in front of an audience.'

As soon as he'd spoken, his hand shot in front of his mouth, as though trying to pull the words back in.

Wait a minute!

'What do you mean . . . *finally*?' asked Vanya.

Mr Le Gonk shook his head. 'I didn't say that.'

'Yes, you did.'

'No, I didn't.'

I don't want to be cruel, but we've already established that Mr Le Gonk is a terrible actor. There was no way we were going to believe him.

Vanya wasn't about to let him get away with it either. She was like a dog with a squeezy toy. 'You've never been onstage before, have you? But you said you were a professional actor. I knew it as soon as I first met you. I googled you and I couldn't find your name anywhere.'

Mr Le Gonk pulled himself up to his full height. 'I am an actor. I *am* an actor!'

From the hall we could hear more applause. The

Year Fives must've finished their song and dance. But we weren't ready to go back just yet.

'All right,' said Vanya, 'what have you been in?'

'Lots of things,' he said, looking hurt.

Vanya folded her arms. 'Name one.'

'Well, I've just been in a major French production, if you must know. I told you that already.'

'What was it called?'

Mr Le Gonk mumbled something that sounded like *minny minny mip*.

From outside we could hear Mrs McDonald calling our names to tell us we were about to go onstage. We ignored her. We heard her tut and her footsteps retreated back to the hall.

'I didn't hear that, sorry,' said Vanya to Mr Le Gonk.

Mr Le Gonk huffed out his cheeks. 'I said . . .' he paused. Vanya raised an eyebrow. 'I said – I was in an advert for oven-cooked French fries. I played –' he took a deep breath – 'a dancing potato.'

I couldn't help myself here. I started laughing.

'See,' he said, slumping down so he was sitting on the ground, 'everyone always laughs at Le Gonk.'

There was a long, awkward pause. Mr Le Gonk

seemed so sad and withered that I actually felt sorry for him.

'I should never have taken this stupid job. Never. I didn't want to teach. I wanted to *act*. But one can't live off baked beans and free oven chips forever. So I signed myself up to a drama teaching agency. And when Rosie's father rang, promising double wages, well . . .'

He sighed and looked sadly at the bottle in his hand. 'Oh, what have I done?' he cried. 'I'm a fool. What kind of monster have I become? Turning people hairy. I should never have come back here.'

Vanya put her hand on his shoulder. 'It was a bit silly, but come on – we all make mistakes,' she said kindly.

'Wait a second,' I said. 'If you aren't an actor, then who are that man and woman? You know, the ones from the TV and film industry who've come to watch Rosie perform.'

Mr Le Gonk gulped guiltily. 'Well . . . er . . . they do work in the film and TV industry, so I technically wasn't lying about that . . .'

'What do they do?' asked Vanya.

'He works for a TV repair shop, and she sells popcorn at the cinema in town.'

'HA!' I said. This was brilliant. Rosie was showing off all her talents to two people, and the only things they could do for her would be to fix her telly and put extra toppings on her popcorn! Fantastic.

'Rosie's father will go mad,' he said.

I didn't bother telling him that he should be more scared of Rosie. When she found out she wasn't going to Hollywood, she'd probably skin him alive.

'Oh no! I've just realised,' said Mr Le Gonk, suddenly. 'What about the cream in the tank? What if . . . ?'

'Don't worry. It's fine,' said Vanya. Now that we knew he was going to be ruining Rosie's dreams, I think that the pair of us were starting to actually like him a little bit. 'The sprinklers will only go off if there's a fire.'

I smiled at Vanya and then at Mr Le Gonk, who smiled sadly back.

'No problem,' she continued. 'We'll tell Mr Noblet. You can come clean. They'll drain the tank. Nobody will become hairy after all. And you can't be *that* terrible if you make Rosie look silly.'

'Thank you, child,' said Mr Le Gonk, climbing

to his feet. 'I don't deserve your kindness. I was a terrible teacher.'

'You certainly were,' said Rosie.

Mr Le Gonk laughed – a great belly laugh that made his whole body shake.

'Maybe you should give the acting another bash,' I said, 'I mean – you've been on telly. Like my mum said, George Moony started out playing a singing satsuma, and he's the most famous actor in the world.'

'You're right,' said Mr Le Gonk. 'I'll do that. And I promise I'll never set foot in a school again!'

Everything was perfect.

For about half a second anyway.

Until a massive KABBOOOOOM!! shook the building, sending tins and boxes rattling off the shelves in the caretaker's cupboard.

'What was that?' panted Mr Le Gonk, holding his heart.

The large tank began to glug. There was a sound of water rushing through the pipes.

I looked at the tank and then at Vanya. I could feel the blood draining from my face.

'Oh no,' she said.

'The sprinklers,' I said.

This could only mean one thing.

'Gamble's mince pie bomb!' we both said together.

We sprinted back towards the hall.

Winter Wonderland

Inside the hall, we were faced with what could only be described as a winter wonderland. Our class were onstage, with Gamble in the middle holding a smouldering foil plate, his face covered in soot and his eyebrows burnt off. Rosie was still dancing at the edge of the stage, staring desperately at the man and woman from the film and TV industry. I didn't have the heart to tell her the truth about them.

Meanwhile, the parents were all on their feet. From somewhere, they'd started singing 'We Wish You a Merry Christmas'.

And what looked like snow was drifting down from the sprinkler system in the ceiling.

Snow. A Christmas snowstorm. Indoors.

Nobody seemed to have noticed that this wasn't normal.

The children were whooping and cheering and

flicking it at each other and grabbing it and rubbing it on their faces like Santa beards.

We knew it wasn't snow though. It was foam. Foam made out of Bald Away mixed with water.

'NOOOO!' cried Vanya.

'Get out!' I screamed at everyone. 'You've got to get out!'

The foam was all over their heads and faces and hands. A few people had even tipped their heads back to catch the foamy flakes on their tongues.

But nobody heard us over the singing and the laughing and the cheering.

Only Mr Noblet and the teachers looked concerned. And they didn't even know what the foam was. They just thought the sprinklers were going off. They were scrambling around, trying to move people outside. But the parents were too busy singing. In fact, they were singing so loudly that you could barely hear the fire alarm.

Vanya and I stood rooted to the spot. There was nothing we could do. And, as everyone in the hall belted out the final chorus, we could see the first sprouts of hair appearing on the first faces.

The mince pies and the actors had finally ruined Christmas.

Epilogue

All in all, around 400 adults and children ended up as furry as I was.

As soon as they realised what was happening, people began gibbering and prodding each other and tugging on their hairy faces and making all these strange howling, hooting noises. It was like being in a roomful of unruly gibbons.

We turned around to Mr Le Gonk, but he was nowhere to be seen. He'd vanished into thin air.

Talk about leaving us in the lurch. When everybody finally calmed down, we had some serious explaining to do to the hairy crowd. I was actually pleased for Mr Le Gonk's sake that he wasn't there. He'd have been torn limb from limb.

The worst person was Rosie. She was hysterical – shrieking and wailing that the TV and film people had seen her as a hairy mess. I cheerfully suggested that they might give her a part in a film about a haunted fur ball that slithers up from a plug hole and strangles people while they're on the toilet. This didn't really make her feel better, but I certainly wasn't about to tell her where the film and TV people *actually* worked.

An ambulance came, and the shocked and overwhelmed paramedics told us that we should all go to the local hospital to be checked out. You should've seen the faces of the people in the waiting room when 400 yetis lumbered in!

It was chaos!

The weird thing was that – even though she now had a long, scruffy beard – Mum was most upset by the fact that she hadn't got to see me perform the 'Brussels Sprout Boogie'.

'It really isn't that good,' I said.

But a couple of other parents had heard her, and they were asking their children too, and within a few minutes there was a clamour of voices begging us to perform.

'I don't think so,' I said, even though most of my classmates seemed ready to go for it.

'If you do it, Roman, you can have one of the treats I bought,' said Mum. 'They're at home in the cupboard.'

'A Squidgy Splodge Chocolate Log Supreme?' I asked.

Mum mumbled something and shoved me towards the rest of my class, and Vanya pulled me to the front.

Mrs McDonald tapped her phone with a hairy finger and the backing music started. Then my class performed the furriest, beardiest and strangest-looking Christmas song of all time.

And so that was that.

Just after we'd finished our performance, and the hairy hand-clapping from our audience had died down, a doctor came out and addressed the room from on top of a chair. It turned out that putting normal hair-removal cream on children isn't a good idea, so the hospital was going to have to order some special mild stuff from abroad. We were all going to be furballs for a while yet.

Rosie Taylor nearly fainted. She was the only one who hadn't performed the song, and her face was covered with a veil. We didn't see her again till after Christmas.

The next week at school, Vanya and I received a postcard from Mr Le Gonk. He apologised for running away but said that he'd had no choice. 'The last time I saw an audience that angry,' he wrote, 'was when I performed *Don't Eat My Toenails* at the Glasgow Empire and Dame Maggie McTurnip dived off the stage and started beating up a coach-load of old people who were breathing too loudly.'

Same old rubbish stories.

Still, he thanked us for persuading him to go back into acting. Apparently, the very next day after running away from our school, he'd been given an 'exciting role', playing a talking pair of boxer shorts in a new kids' TV show called *Doctor Grundy's Incredible Undies*.

I think I'll give it a miss when it comes on telly.

And as for the 'treat' Mum gave me when we got back from the hospital – was it a Chocolate Log Supreme?

Was it heck.

It was a flipping mince pie.

Piccadilly

PRESS

Thank you for choosing a Piccadilly Press book.

If you would like to know more about our authors, our books or if you'd just like to know what we're up to, you can find us online.

www.piccadillypress.co.uk

And you can also find us on:

We hope to see you soon!